NO

ONE

THERE

(a sofia blake fbi suspense thriller —book 1)

a v a   s t r o n g

Ava Strong

Ava Strong is author of the REMI LAURENT mystery series, comprising six books (and counting); of the ILSE BECK mystery series, comprising seven books (and counting); of the STELLA FALL psychological suspense thriller series, comprising six books (and counting); of the DAKOTA STEELE FBI suspense thriller series, comprising six books (and counting); of the LILY DAWN suspense thriller series, comprising five books (and counting); the MEGAN YORK FBI suspense thriller series, comprising five books (and counting); and the SOFIA BLAKE FBI suspense thriller series, comprising five books (and counting).

An avid reader and lifelong fan of the mystery and thriller genres, Ava loves to hear from you, so please feel free to visit www.avastrongauthor.com to learn more and stay in touch.

NOT LIKE BEFORE (Book #6)
NOT LIKE NORMAL (Book #7)

STELLA FALL PSYCHOLOGICAL SUSPENSE THRILLER
HIS OTHER WIFE (Book #1)
HIS OTHER LIE (Book #2)
HIS OTHER SECRET (Book #3)
HIS OTHER MISTRESS (Book #4)
HIS OTHER LIFE (Book #5)
HIS OTHER TRUTH (Book #6)

DAKOTA STEELE FBI SUSPENSE THRILLER
WITHOUT MERCY (Book #1)
WITHOUT REMORSE (Book #2)
WITHOUT A PAST (Book #3)
WITHOUT PITY (Book #4)
WITHOUT HOPE (Book #5)

PROLOGUE

Alberto and Mateo dashed down the cobblestone street, their sneakers pounding against the uneven stones. The soccer ball they chased seemed to dance between them, teasing at their determination to outdo one another.

"You won't get past me, Alberto," Mateo taunted, panting slightly as he blocked his friend's next attempt.

"Watch me!" Alberto shot back, eyes narrowed with unwavering focus.

La Porta, California, was alive with the vibrant colors and sounds of Día de los Muertos, the Day of the Dead festival. Paper banners bearing intricate designs fluttered above the streets, casting dancing shadows on the throngs of people below. Laughter and lively conversation mingled with the enticing aromas of street food as vendors hawked their wares, their voices rising above the festive din. Marigolds adorned every surface, their deep orange petals a symbol of the sun, guiding the spirits of the deceased back to the world of the living for this annual celebration.

People of all ages wandered through the streets, faces painted with elaborate skull designs that mirrored the calaveras – sugar skulls – displayed in shop windows. Children clutched bags of sweets, their eyes wide with wonder at the festivities; grandparents sat on benches, watching the world pass by with knowing smiles. Catrinas – the elegantly dressed female skeletons that had become synonymous with the holiday – posed for photos, their skirts swirling around them like vivid clouds.

"Hey! Keep up!" Mateo called to Alberto, who had momentarily been lost in the scene unfolding around him. He shook himself from his reverie and sprinted after Mateo, caught up in the thrill of the game once more.

As the ball flew through the air and veered off course, Alberto's heart skipped a beat. He and Mateo sprinted after it. The ball careened toward an older man, who intercepted it with a swift kick, sending it bouncing away from them.

"Hey!" Mateo shouted, his voice laced with indignation.

The older man, with deep-set eyes that glinted like steel in the early sunlight, glared at them. His face was weathered and lined, like an old map with countless tales to tell. As he turned away, Alberto could see the gray hair that peeked out from under his wide-brimmed hat, matching the thick mustache that framed his thin lips.

"Who does he think he is?" Mateo muttered as they fetched the ball, his words dripping with annoyance.

Alberto frowned. "I don't know, but he didn't need to be so rude."

"Wouldn't it be funny if we followed him and robbed him?" Mateo suggested, his mischievous grin spreading across his face like wildfire.

"Are you crazy? My mom would kill me if she found out." Alberto's eyes darted around nervously, as if his mother might materialize from the shadows.

"Come on, it'll be fun—just this one time." The excitement in Mateo's eyes was as bright as a pair of fireflies.

"Alright," Alberto finally agreed, feeling a mixture of exhilaration and trepidation churn within him. "But only because he was so mean to us."

"Deal!" Mateo exclaimed, slapping Alberto on the back. "Now let's follow him and make sure we stay close."

As the boys trailed behind the older man, Alberto's heart hammered against his chest, each beat a reminder of the dangerous game they were about to play. He tried to focus on the task at hand, but the vibrant sights and sounds of the Día de los Muertos festival threatened to distract him. The scent of marigolds hung heavy in the air, mingling with the aroma of sweet pastries and spiced cocoa.

"Remember," Mateo whispered, his voice low and serious, "he deserves this. Maybe this'll teach him a lesson."

Alberto nodded, swallowing hard as he steeled himself for what was to come.

They wove through the crowd, trying to keep up with their target without being noticed. Alberto felt a pang of guilt at their devious plan. He'd never done anything quite like this before, but Mateo had. Mateo's friends were always dragging him into trouble, and in turn Mateo dragged Alberto into trouble.

He's a bad influence, Alberto heard his mother say. *Always causing problems.* Alberto wondered if he should have listened to his mother this time. It was too late now, however. They'd already caught up to the older man.

"Alright," Mateo whispered as they drew closer to their unsuspecting target, "I'll distract him while you try to pick his pocket."

He gave Alberto a conspiratorial wink before adding, "Make sure to be quick and quiet."

Before Alberto could protest, Mateo dashed forward with a sudden burst of energy, narrowly avoiding a group of elaborately costumed revelers. He pretended to trip, falling into the older man with a well-executed stumble.

"Oof! I'm so sorry, señor!" Mateo exclaimed, feigning embarrassment as he clung to the man's arm for balance. The older man raised an eyebrow, but didn't say anything.

Seizing the opportunity, Alberto moved in closer, his fingers trembling with nervous anticipation. As he reached for the man's pocket, his hand bumped against something hard and cold. Panic rose within him as he realized what it was—a gun. His breath caught in his throat, and his mind raced.

What have we gotten ourselves into? he thought.

The older man, sensing the intrusion, turned his glare upon Alberto. With a swift motion, he tried to grab the boy by the collar, but Alberto, propelled by adrenaline, slipped away just in time. He sprinted toward the nearest alley, his heart pounding in his ears.

"Run!" he shouted, urging Mateo to follow suit. Mateo, still grinning devilishly, threw a cheeky wave in the older man's direction before dashing off after Alberto.

As they disappeared into the shadows of the alley, the older man's snarl faded behind them, a chilling reminder of the danger they had narrowly escaped.

Gasping for breath, the boys slowed to a stop. They looked at one another for a moment, their faces serious. Then, at the same time, they both burst into laughter.

With a grin, Mateo revealed his prize: a gleaming gold watch, snatched from the older man's wrist during their daring escape.

"Look what I got!" he said triumphantly, holding it up for Alberto to see. At first, worry clouded Alberto's face, but soon he couldn't help but laugh along with his friend.

"His face—did you see his face?" Alberto wheezed between bouts of laughter. "He looked like he'd seen a ghost!"

"Yeah!" Mateo agreed, eyes sparkling with mischief. "Too bad we didn't get more, though."

"More? Are you crazy?" Alberto said, the lingering adrenaline making him bold. "We're lucky that's all we got! That guy had a gun, Mateo!"

"Wow, really?" Mateo whistled, his eyebrows raised in surprise. "Well, at least we got this fancy watch out of it. We can sell it and make some good money."

"Maybe...but my mom would kill me if she found out," Alberto muttered, his thoughts already drifting toward the possible consequences of their actions.

"Ah, don't worry about it," Mateo said, slapping his friend on the back. "We'll figure something out."

As they continued farther into the shadows, the laughter faded, replaced by an uneasy silence. The alley was darker than Alberto had anticipated, and he strained his eyes to navigate the unfamiliar terrain.

Suddenly he stumbled, his foot catching on something. His heart leapt into his throat as he peered into the darkness, trying to discern the source of his fright.

"Qué demonios?" he whispered, staring at a pair of legs sticking out from beside a dumpster, just barely visible in the gloom. Fear gripped him, and he felt a cold sweat break out across his brow. "Mateo...there's someone here."

"Probably just a *borracha* sleeping it off," Mateo said dismissively, though his voice held a note of uncertainty. His eyes scanned the area warily, still not completely at ease.

"Maybe...but why would they be hiding here?" Alberto couldn't keep the tremor from his voice as a thousand terrible possibilities raced through his mind.

"Who knows? People do weird stuff when they're drunk." Mateo attempted to laugh, but the sound was hollow, devoid of its usual carefree nature.

Cautiously, Alberto approached the figure sprawled next to the dumpster. As he drew closer, the details of the woman came into focus. Her raven hair spilled over her face in disarray, and her once-vibrant makeup had been smeared and streaked across her cheeks. A sugar skull adorned with strange symbols lay upon her chest, a macabre centerpiece that seemed out of place amongst the surrounding filth.

"Look at her eyes," Mateo whispered, his earlier bravado reduced to a quivering breath. The woman's gaze was fixed on some distant point, wide-eyed and unseeing. "She's not blinking... Do you think she's okay?"

"Maybe she's just passed out?" Alberto suggested, though his voice carried no conviction. It wasn't like any *borracha* he'd ever seen before, and the bizarre scene sent shivers down his spine.

"Hey, lady!" Mateo called out hesitantly, taking a step closer. *"Estás bien?"*

When she didn't respond, Alberto felt a morbid fascination take hold of him, urging him forward. He knelt next to the motionless woman, his heart pounding in his ears. His hand shook as he reached out, placing two trembling fingers on the side of her neck.

Mateo hung back, unwilling to come any closer.

Alberto swallowed hard, his throat tight. "She's not breathing," he whispered.

"¿Qué? No puede ser..." Mateo's eyes grew wider, his fear now mirrored in Alberto's own.

It was then that Alberto noticed it—the gash in the woman's throat, a dark crimson stain against her pale skin. His stomach churned as bile rose in his throat, the implications of what they had stumbled upon crashing down around him like a tidal wave.

He stepped back in horror, unable to put words to the discovery. Then, finally, he let out a scream.

The skull, untroubled, went on grinning.

CHAPTER ONE

Patience, Special Agent Sofia Blake told herself. *They'll recognize your value soon enough.*

She was standing in a dimly lit CIA room, her gaze fixed on the large monitor that dominated one wall. The screen displayed rapidly scrolling lines of code representing a monetary transaction between a known terrorist and an unknown accomplice. Surrounding her, half-hidden in the shadows, were high-ranking officials, their expressions grave as they silently watched the unfolding scene.

At the center of it all, a young coder sat hunched over a computer, his fingers flying across the keyboard as he desperately tried to keep up with the information on the screen. Beads of sweat glistened on his forehead, and his breathing came in shallow gasps. Sofia couldn't help but notice the stark contrast between the young man's pale complexion and the dark, tailored suit that clung to his wiry frame. He was clearly overwhelmed, yet no one seemed willing to step in and offer assistance.

Hovering by the coder's elbow was his supervisor, a tall, imposing man with salt-and-pepper hair and cold, calculating eyes. His arms were crossed over his broad chest, and his gaze never left the screen. Every few seconds, he would shoot the coder a sidelong glance that seemed to say, *You're not doing this fast enough.* His very presence added an oppressive weight to the air, ratcheting up the tension in the room.

Sofia took a deep breath and let it out slowly, doing her best to keep her frustration in check. It was absurd that the CIA had invited her to assist with this operation only to relegate her to the sidelines while their own coder floundered. Her coding skills were, after all, the reason the CIA had invited her to take part in this investigation in the first place. Though she much preferred the languages of human beings to that of computers, she had an aptitude for all languages. Her mind picked up patterns with an ease that had never been rivaled in her experience, making automatic connections at a speed others often found dizzying. This was how she had become an expert in her field, earning linguistic degrees from Harvard, Berkeley, and other top universities. She might have stayed an academic the rest of her life, following in the footsteps of her parents, if her eventual partner, Ryan Donovan, hadn't tracked her down to assist in catching the Code Killer, a serial killer whose cryptic messages had baffled investigators for years before Sofia managed to decode them.

This kid's in over his head, she thought, feeling sorry for the young coder as he struggled to process the ever-changing streams of data on the screen. Sofia knew better than to voice her concerns aloud, however. In this room full of self-important officials, her opinion would likely fall on deaf ears.

As the code continued to flow across the screen like a turbulent river, Sofia sensed that time was running out. If something didn't change soon, they would lose their window of opportunity to intercept the funds and apprehend the terrorists. She knew she had the skills and experience to make a difference, if only they would let her. But for now, all she could do was watch as the young coder's frantic attempts grew increasingly futile, and hope that someone would recognize the need for action before it was too late.

A voice broke through her thoughts.

"Are you going to do anything, Agent Blake?" the supervisor snapped, his impatience palpable as he glared at her.

Sofia turned her gaze toward him, her lips pursed in a thin line. "You told me to be quiet until you asked for my help," she replied coolly. "So I'm remaining quiet."

"Well, you might as well give this a shot. Toby here has clearly reached his limit."

With a slow, deliberate stride, Sofia approached the computer where the young coder, Toby, was working. His fingers were a blur on the keyboard, the relentless tapping almost rhythmic despite the ever-changing code that filled the screen. He was good, Sofia had to admit—but not good enough.

"Move aside," the supervisor ordered Toby, his voice cold and commanding.

"Wait." Sofia raised a hand, silencing him. "He stays. He's quicker with the keys than I am. He'll type, I'll dictate."

"Very well," the supervisor conceded with a skeptical frown, stepping back to give her room.

As Sofia studied the rapidly shifting data, her mind whirred into motion. She felt the familiar surge of adrenaline as her brain began making connections, deciphering the complex web before her. Her heart raced in tandem with the coder's keystrokes, each beat propelling her closer to the solution they so desperately needed.

"Alright," she said, taking a deep breath. "Let's begin."

Her eyes narrowed as she focused on the information displayed across multiple screens, the electric blue of the code casting a dim glow on her face. The room seemed to fade away as she absorbed the intricate patterns and minute details within the data stream. She was like an impenetrable fortress, her mind rapidly making connections, tracking multiple streams of information simultaneously.

"Start with the third line," she said, her voice steady and confident. "Replace the '@' symbol with 'X,' and move the entire block two spaces to the left."

The coder's fingers flew across the keyboard, executing her commands with precision. He glanced up at her in gratitude as she effortlessly navigated the labyrinthine code.

"Excellent," she murmured, her gaze never leaving the screen. "Now, switch the first and second letters of every fourth word, starting from the top."

As Toby began typing, Sofia's mind continued to process the information before her. It was as if she were both conductor and orchestra, harmonizing the cacophony of symbols and phrases into a symphony of clarity. At times, it seemed she could process the information as quickly as the computer itself, her linguistic prowess shining through.

"Reverse the order of the numbers in the fifth row," she said. "Then multiply each by seven and add three."

Her thoughts raced ahead, anticipating the next series of changes required to decipher the code. With each new connection, the puzzle unraveled further, revealing its secrets piece by piece. The room was enveloped in silence, save for the rhythmic tapping of the coder's fingers and Sofia's hushed instructions.

"Change every occurrence of 'Y' to 'Z,' and then shift all punctuation marks one space to the right," she added. As the coder made the adjustments, Sofia could feel the solution drawing near, like a distant light growing brighter with each passing moment.

"Finally," she said, a hint of triumph in her voice, "replace all instances of 'Q' with the square root symbol, and move the entire last paragraph up four spaces."

The coder hesitated for just a moment, his fingers hovering over the keys as if to confirm he'd heard her correctly. Then, with a final flourish, he entered the last command.

The code morphed before their eyes, transforming into a comprehensible message laden with critical information. Sofia allowed herself a small, satisfied smile as the supervisor stared at the screen, dumbfounded by her prowess. They could finally move forward, armed with the knowledge they had so desperately sought.

"Good work," she said softly, giving the young coder a nod of approval before turning her attention back to the task at hand. There was still much to be done, but now they had a fighting chance. And in this deadly game of cat and mouse, every advantage counted.

The supervisor's eyes widened with astonishment as he watched Sofia work her magic. She had taken command of the situation, her confidence and expertise both soothing and shocking the room full of tense officials. She felt like a painter skillfully bringing a blank canvas to life, each stroke revealing more and more of the hidden masterpiece.

"Alright," she said, addressing the coder. "Now that we have a clear understanding of the transaction, we need to flag the money being exchanged." Her gaze shifted to another screen displaying the grainy footage of a security camera. "I also want you to dispatch agents to this location. There's one more thing—trigger the sprinkler system."

The young coder hesitated, glancing at the supervisor for confirmation. He simply nodded, still visibly awed by Sofia's abilities.

"Trust me," Sofia added softly, her eyes never leaving the screen as she analyzed the unfolding scene. "The sprinklers will lock down the bulletproof doors and trap the suspects inside."

The coder swallowed hard, his fingers dancing across the keyboard in response to Sofia's instructions. Within minutes, several windows popped up on the screen, confirming that the agents had been dispatched and the sprinkler system activated. The monetary transfer was successfully flagged, ensuring that it could be traced back to its origin.

Sofia's heart pounded in her chest as she observed the rapidly changing situation. With each passing second, the terrorists were moving closer to capture, and the weight of responsibility pressed down on her shoulders like a thousand-pound boulder. She knew every decision she made could mean the difference between life or death— not just for the agents being sent into the field, but for countless innocent people who might find themselves caught in the crossfire.

Her mind raced, juggling multiple streams of information as she tried to anticipate the terrorists' next moves. She needed to stay one step ahead of them, to outthink and outmaneuver them at every turn. It was a challenge she had faced many times before, but the stakes had never been higher.

"Keep an eye on these coordinates," she instructed the young coder, her voice steady, even as adrenaline coursed through her veins. "If anything changes, let me know immediately."

As Sofia watched the scene unfold on the grainy screen, her thoughts flickered like shadows in the dimly lit room. She knew that the coming minutes would determine the outcome of this deadly game—and whether or not she could claim victory for herself and her team.

The seconds ticked by like a ticking bomb, the tension in the room thickening with each passing moment. Sofia's eyes remained fixated on the screen, her heart pounding in anticipation. The agents she had dispatched moved stealthily through the dimly lit building, their every movement captured on the live feed.

"Target sighted," one agent whispered into his communication device, his voice low and taut with determination. Sofia felt her pulse quicken as the moment of reckoning approached.

"Proceed with caution," she instructed, her voice betraying no hint of the turmoil within her. She knew that one wrong move could end in disaster, and it was her responsibility to ensure the success of this operation.

As the agents closed in on the terrorists, the room around Sofia held its breath. The officials who had silently observed the proceedings now leaned closer to the screens, their expressions a mix of awe and anxiety. Even the supervisor, who had initially doubted Sofia's capabilities, watched with rapt attention.

"Remember the plan," Sofia said quietly, more to herself than anyone else. "Trust your instincts."

The arrest happened almost too quickly for anyone to comprehend. A sudden flurry of movement on the screen, shouts that echoed through the communication devices, and then...silence. The terrorists had been apprehended, and Sofia felt the weight on her shoulders lift ever so slightly.

"Amazing," the supervisor said, shaking his head in disbelief. Around him, the room erupted into murmurs of astonishment and admiration. Sofia, however, simply smiled—a small, satisfied curl of her lips that spoke volumes about her quiet confidence.

"Thank you," she said, accepting the praise with grace. In truth, it wasn't the adulation she sought, but the knowledge that she had used her skills to protect innocent lives and bring criminals to justice. That was the true reward for her tireless efforts.

As she turned to leave the room, her phone rang, its jarring tone slicing through the lingering buzz of excitement. She glanced at the screen and saw the letters "FBI" flash before her eyes.

"Hello?" she answered, her voice steady even as her mind raced with possibilities.

The voice of her FBI partner, Ryan Donovan, filled her ear. "You still helping out with that terrorist thing?" he asked.

"Just wrapped it up," she said, a note of pride creeping into her voice. "All in a day's work."

"Well, good timing, then, because the boss has something new for us. He wants you back here ASAP."

"What is it?" she asked, her brow creasing.

"A double homicide—and it sounds like this one is right up your alley."

CHAPTER TWO

The cool November air whipped through Sofia's hair as she cruised down the street, relishing the feeling of triumph that still lingered from her recent victory over the CIA officials.

She loved proving people wrong, especially those who had underestimated her throughout her career. As an ambitious and determined woman in a male-dominated field, it was moments like these that fueled her fire and reminded her why she loved what she did for a living.

She guided her sleek, black Dodge Charger into the parking lot of the FBI headquarters in San Francisco. The car was just as powerful and unyielding as she was, and she took pride in the way it caught the attention of passersby. She parked it with precision, admiring the way her vehicle stood out among the sea of dull, government-issued sedans.

As she stepped out of the car, the cool wind picked up strands of her dark hair, sending them dancing around her face. She looked up at the imposing FBI building, its glass façade brilliantly reflecting the early sun. Seagulls called to each other overhead, their cries mingling with the distant hum of traffic and the faint, salty scent of the ocean nearby.

People hurried along, bundled in their coats and scarves, each wrapped up in their own problems and concerns. Sofia could sense the undercurrents of tension that rippled through the crowd, reflecting the ever-present dangers that lurked beneath the surface of everyday life.

She walked across the parking lot, her heels clicking against the pavement with authority. The wind continued to toy with her hair, but she paid no mind as she neared the entrance to the FBI building. Her thoughts were already on the tasks ahead: meetings, briefings, and the never-ending pursuit of justice. It was a pursuit that she thrived on, fueled by her desire to prove herself—not just to others, but to herself as well.

As she neared the entrance of the FBI building, her eyes were drawn to a man leaning against a red Chevy Silverado. The car's polished exterior glistened in the weak November sunlight, its sharp angles and tinted windows giving it an air of mystery. The man himself was tall and broad-shouldered, his blond hair cut short and a hint of stubble shadowing his strong jawline. It was her partner, Ryan Donovan.

"Word travels fast," he said with a disapproving frown as she approached. "I heard about your little performance at the CIA base."

Sofia's heart skipped a beat, but before she could respond, Ryan's frown morphed into a wide grin. "You sure showed those pencil-pushers who's boss."

"Someone had to remind them that they're not the only ones in town with brains," Sofia said, a small smile playing on her lips.

She and Ryan had known each other for over five years now, ever since Ryan had transferred from the New York office to join the San Francisco branch. Their partnership had been one of mutual respect and trust from the beginning, each recognizing the other's dedication to their work and their shared passion for justice.

Over time, their friendship had grown, evolving into something more profound than simple camaraderie. They understood each other in a way few others did, sharing jokes and confidences while navigating the high-pressure world of federal law enforcement. While there was no romance between them, Sofia held a deep respect for Ryan, admiring his intelligence, his unwavering moral compass, and his ability to stay calm under pressure.

"Well," Ryan said, pushing off from the truck and thrusting his hands into his pockets, "we'd better not keep the boss waiting. You know how he gets." He raised his eyebrows, and Sofia let out a low, mirthless chuckle. Oh, yes. She knew how grumpy their boss could be.

They climbed the steps together in companionable silence. As they entered the building, the heavy glass doors of the FBI headquarters closed behind them, muffling the noise of the bustling city. The ordered interior was a stark contrast to the chaos outside, with sleek marble floors reflecting the overhead fluorescent lighting, casting a sterile glow over everything.

"Feels like home, doesn't it?" Ryan joked as they walked past the metal detectors and security checkpoint.

Sofia rolled her eyes but couldn't suppress a small smile. "Don't tempt me. Sometimes I wonder if I should just have a bunk room here so I can save on gas."

"Hey, don't knock it till you try it," Ryan replied, his grin widening.

As they made their way through the labyrinthine hallways, the hum of activity was palpable. Agents huddled in groups, discussing cases, and sharing intelligence, while others hurried past them, their faces etched with determination. The faint aroma of coffee wafted through the air, mingling with the scent of printer ink and well-worn leather.

The pair continued down the hallway until they reached the door to their boss's office. Ryan was recounting a particularly amusing story about their last undercover assignment, laughter dancing in his eyes.

"And then," he was saying, "the perp just looked at me and said, 'You're not a real drug dealer, are you?'"

Sofia laughed, shaking her head. "You're a terrible actor, Ryan. I don't know how you even managed to get through that assignment."

Ryan grinned. "I have my ways."

They knocked on the door, and a gruff voice called out, "Enter."

Sofia was still smiling at Ryan's story. As she pushed open the door and stepped inside the office, however, her mirth evaporated in an instant.

Behind a large mahogany desk sat Leon Hayes, his brow furrowed and his lips pressed into a thin line. The room itself was spacious and well-appointed, its walls adorned with framed certificates and commendations that bore witness to Hayes's long and distinguished career. He was smiling in many of the pictures, but he was not smiling now.

"Agent Blake, Agent Donovan," Leon said curtly, his voice saturated with disapproval. "Please, have a seat."

Sofia felt the weight of her boss's gaze bearing down on her as she took a seat across from him, her posture stiff and her hands folded neatly in her lap. She could sense Ryan's concern for her as he sat down beside her, but she refused to let the tension show on her face.

"Agent Blake," Leon began, his voice cold and authoritative, "I heard about your little performance at the CIA base today." He paused, staring Sofia down with icy blue eyes. "Showboating has no place in our line of work."

Sofia clenched her jaw, fighting the urge to snap back. Instead, she opted for a more controlled approach. "Sir, I was doing my job. If my actions led to a breakthrough—"

"Enough!" Leon's voice boomed through the office.

Sofia swallowed hard, her frustration simmering beneath the surface. She had always felt that Leon harbored some sort of grudge against her, though she couldn't quite pinpoint why. Was it because she was a woman in a male-dominated field or was there something else? Whatever the reason, she refused to let him break her spirit.

"The truth is, Agent Blake," Leon continued, his tone slightly softer but still stern, "I am growing wary of your tendency to put on a show for others."

Sofia caught the misuse of "wary" instead of "weary" but chose not to comment on it. As someone who had memorized more than one dictionary, she had a keen ear for linguistic errors. However, she knew better than to correct her boss in the heat of the moment.

"I expect professionalism from all of my agents," Leon added, his gaze never leaving Sofia's face. "I don't want to hear any more reports about you drawing unnecessary attention to yourself or this agency."

"Understood, sir," Sofia replied. Her mind raced with thoughts of how she could have handled the situation differently, but she knew that dwelling on the past wouldn't change the present. It was time to focus on the work at hand and put this confrontation behind her.

Ryan cleared his throat. "Now that that's settled, perhaps we should discuss the new case?"

Leon shot Sofia a final warning glance before turning on the monitor mounted on the wall. The screen displayed two gruesome images of women lying dead in dark alleys, their throats brutally slashed open. "These victims were found in a small town called La Porta not far south of here," he began, clicking through slides as he spoke. "The first body was discovered two days ago, and the second early this morning."

"What were their names?" Sofia asked.

"Roberta Lima and Jessenia Arjona. Lima was discovered first."

As her eyes scanned the morbid scene, Sofia noticed an intricate sugar skull resting on the second victim's chest. She stepped closer, intrigued.

Ryan cocked his head. "What is that?"

"It's a calavera," she said. "A sugar skull used during Día de los Muertos, the Day of the Dead. Today and tomorrow, November first and second, are the days it's celebrated."

Her fingers involuntarily traced the edge of the table, the cold surface grounding her as she recalled the vibrant festivities she had witnessed during her time in Mexico. The air there had been filled with the scent of marigolds and the sounds of laughter, a stark contrast to the somber reality of the images before her now. She could almost taste the sweet *pan de muerto*, the bread of the dead, a traditional offering for the deceased loved ones.

"Interesting," Ryan murmured, his gaze never leaving the haunting images on the screen. "What does it mean? Why would the killer leave that skull on the victim's body?"

Sofia's brow furrowed, her mind racing with possibilities. The calavera was a reminder of life's fleeting nature and a celebration of those who had passed, but its presence on the victim's body twisted it into something sinister. "I can't be certain," she admitted, her voice not much louder than the hum of the office's air conditioning. "But it's definitely connected to Día de los Muertos. Whoever killed her, they clearly did so on this particular day for a reason."

Leon clicked the remote, and the next image filled the screen—a close-up of the calavera. The sugar skull was intricately adorned with strange symbols that seemed to dance along its surface like shadows cast by flickering candlelight.

"Looks like some sort of code," Ryan muttered, his brow furrowing as he scrutinized the image.

Sofia leaned in, her eyes narrowing as she studied the symbols. "It's not a code," she said after a moment. "It's more like...someone with a poor grasp of Nahuatl."

Leon threw her an impatient glance, clearly irritated by her expertise. "Nahuatl?" he asked, his tone betraying his weariness.

"It's an Aztec language," Sofia explained, noting the way Leon's jaw clenched at her words. She couldn't help but feel satisfaction in being able to provide information he didn't already know.

Ryan raised his eyebrows, impressed. "You know Nahuatl? Where'd you learn that?"

Sofia opened her mouth to answer, reminiscing about the time she had spent in Mexico during her linguistics studies, when Leon suddenly cut her off, his voice terse and commanding. "That's not important right now. What matters is getting to La Porta as soon as possible. There's no telling what our killer will do next."

The stark urgency in Leon's voice sent a shiver down Sofia's spine, forcing her thoughts back to the present. She shot Ryan a sidelong glance, catching the concern mirrored in his eyes. They both knew they were racing against the clock.

"Of course," she said, nodding. "We'll get on it right away."

As she retreated to the door, followed by Ryan, it occurred to her that Leon may very well have hit the nail on the head. Día de los Muertos only lasted two days, so if the killer had some private reason to commit murders during this festival, then his time was limited.

And there was no telling how many bodies he might leave before the festival ended.

CHAPTER THREE

Día de los Muertos, Sofia thought, feeling a chill as she stared through the windshield at the crowd gathered in the street. *For one person, the name has a much more sinister meaning. But is he still here, or has he already accomplished his purpose and left?*

Despite her unease, Sofia couldn't be troubled for long. The atmosphere of La Porta was electric, the streets teeming with life and color, despite the somber undertone that pervaded the small California town. The locals had embraced the ancient festival with fervor, adorning their homes and businesses with marigolds, papel picado banners, and elaborate sugar skulls.

If these people knew about the murders, it didn't seem to be doing anything to dampen the mood.

"Amazing, isn't it?" she said to Ryan as they climbed out of her Dodge Charger and paused to survey the festive scene before them.

"Can't say I really know what it's about," Ryan said, scratching the back of his neck even as his eyes narrowed thoughtfully. "I know it has something to do with the dead, but..."

"It's a time for families to honor their deceased loved ones, to remember them, and celebrate their lives," Sofia explained. "That's why it's about fun and joy, not grief."

She thought of the festival's origins in the Aztec civilization, its later fusion with the Catholic All Saints' Day and All Souls' Day, and the myriad customs and traditions that had evolved over the centuries. She decided Ryan didn't need all that information at the moment, however.

"¡Amigos, amigos!" a vendor called out to them from his stall, a dazzling array of intricately decorated calaveras spread out before him. *"¿Te gustaría ver nuestras calaveras de azúcar?"*

"Claro," Sofia replied without missing a beat, her Spanish flawless and flowing. *"Nos encantaría verlas."*

"Wow," Ryan murmured, clearly impressed by her linguistic prowess. "I should probably know this by now, but exactly how many languages do you speak?"

Sofia grinned, momentarily basking in the praise. "A few," she said modestly. "Spanish, French, Italian, Russian... Languages have always fascinated me. They're like puzzle pieces, and when you fit them together, they create a beautiful tapestry of human history and culture."

They wandered over to the vendor's stall and took a moment to examine the calaveras on display. Some of the skulls resembled famous politicians and celebrities, while others looked like beloved pets, all made from colorful sugar and vibrant icing.

As they browsed, the hairs on the back of Sofia's neck began to stand up without warning. She froze, her smile tightening.

"What is it?" Ryan asked, leaning close.

"Just have the odd feeling we're being watched."

She stole a look around, but she didn't see any eyes looking back. Strange. Still, it was a good reminder that they hadn't come here just to enjoy the festivities.

She thanked the vendor and they moved on farther down the street. The cacophony of the festival seemed to fade away as her gaze was drawn to an alley sectioned off with caution tape. The sharp contrast between the vibrant street and the narrow, dark alleyway sent a shiver down her spine. She exchanged a glance with Ryan before they both ducked beneath the tape.

The alley was suffocating in its narrowness, the tall buildings on either side casting long shadows that gave the impression of being swallowed by darkness. A faint odor of decay and dampness lingered in the air, tainting the sweet smells from the festival outside. Several police officers stood huddled together, murmuring among themselves as they cast uneasy glances at the crime scene.

"Excuse me," Sofia said. It felt wrong to disturb the eerie silence that hung over the alley like a shroud.

A tall woman with short, curly hair and piercing blue eyes turned to face Sofia. Her uniform was impeccably neat, complete with a shiny badge that glinted in what little sunlight managed to filter through the gloom.

"Detective Garcia," she introduced herself, extending a hand. "You must be Special Agents Blake and Donovan. We've been expecting you."

"Nice to meet you," Sofia replied, shaking her hand. "What can you tell us about the scene?"

Detective Garcia hesitated for a moment, her gaze drifting back to the center of the alley. "Miss Arjona was found beside this dumpster. The body has been removed, but there's still...this." She pointed to a sugar skull resting on the ground, untouched since its discovery.

As Sofia's eyes fell upon the calavera, she felt a cold, sinking feeling in the pit of her stomach. It was beautiful in its macabre elegance, the intricate patterns, and colors a stark reminder of the fusion of life and death that lay at the heart of Día de los Muertos. And yet, here it was, a symbol of celebration turned into an instrument of terror.

"Who found the body?" Ryan asked, his voice steady despite the grim scene before them.

"Couple of kids were the first to come across the body," Detective Garcia replied, then grunted. "Probably were up to no good, snooping around back here. They came screaming out like banshees, and a nearby shopkeeper decided to investigate. Poor guy's still shaken up—probably be having nightmares for a while."

So will those kids, Sofia thought, shaking her head sadly.

She knelt beside the calavera, her fingers hovering just above the surface as she traced the unfamiliar symbols etched into its delicate frame. The cool alley air seemed to cling to her skin, the hairs on her arms prickling with unease. She felt Ryan's gaze on her, heavy with expectation.

"Can you read what it says?" he asked.

Before she could answer, another voice interrupted, smooth and confident. "Of course she can't read it. The symbols don't make any sense."

Sofia turned her head sharply, eyes locking onto the figure that had emerged from the shadows of the alley. He was lithe and athletic, with dark hair that fell casually across his forehead. His smile was warm and inviting, a stark contrast to the chill that hung in the air.

There was an undeniable charm about him, one that seemed to defy the grim scene that surrounded them.

"I'm sorry," Ryan said, "but who are you?"

"Ah, apologies for my intrusion," the man replied, holding up his hands in a placating gesture. "My name is Ethan Knight. I was called in to assist with this case. I'd like to think it's because of my rakish good looks, but it probably has more to do with my PhD in Mesoamerican languages." He winked at Sofia.

Sofia's curiosity piqued at the mention of his studies. She loved languages, and the idea of someone specializing in something so unique and niche fascinated her. "That's incredible," she said, unable to keep the admiration from her voice. "What drew you to that particular field?"

Ethan's eyes seemed to light up, his grin widening. "Well, I've always been captivated by ancient cultures and their means of communication. The history, the artistry...it's all so fascinating. And Mesoamerican languages, especially, hold a certain allure, don't you think?"

As they spoke, Sofia found herself drawn in by Ethan's passion and knowledge. It was rare to find someone who shared her enthusiasm for languages, and she couldn't help but feel a flicker of excitement amid the grim circumstances.

"Can you tell us anything about these symbols?" Ryan interjected before Sofia and Ethan could get sidetracked any further. Sofia felt a flush creep up her cheeks as she realized how easily she had been distracted.

"Unfortunately, no," Ethan admitted, his brow furrowing as he studied the calavera once more. "The symbols are authentic, but the arrangement...it's nonsensical."

Sofia wasn't so sure, though. There was something about the arrangement of the glyphs that niggled at the back of her mind, like a half-remembered melody. Her eyes traced the intricate lines, searching for some elusive pattern. But she couldn't prove it yet.

"Wait," she murmured, leaning closer to the skull. "Look at this."

Ethan and Ryan peered over her shoulder, their breaths warm puffs of air against her skin. She pointed to a particularly ornate glyph, her finger hovering just above the delicate calligraphy.

"See how the lines are perfectly straight? And how the curves are smooth, almost machine-like?" she asked, her voice hushed with excitement. "This wasn't done by hand. It's too precise, too uniform. It must've been done with a laser engraver."

Ethan's eyes widened, clearly impressed. "Incredible," he said. "I hadn't even considered that possibility. But you're right, the level of detail is extraordinary."

Ryan nodded, his brow furrowed in concentration. "That could be an important lead, then. Whoever engraved these symbols must have access to specialized equipment."

A shiver ran down Sofia's spine as she continued to study the skull, the implications of her discovery sinking in. The killer had gone to great lengths to craft this intricate calling card, but why? What message were they trying to convey?

The wind picked up, swirling around Sofia as she continued to study the intricate calligraphy on the calavera. The laser-engraved symbols still eluded her understanding, but she couldn't shake the nagging feeling that there was a hidden pattern just beyond her grasp.

"Hey," Ryan said, breaking into her thoughts. "Maybe we should look into what kind of machines could create these engravings. They can't all be the same, right?"

Sofia glanced at him, then back at the skull. She could see the delicate swoops and curves of the symbols, their precision and intricacy both beautiful and chilling. "That's not a bad idea," she said. "If we can identify the machine used, it might lead us to whoever created this."

Ethan nodded, his eyes taking on a determined glint. "I have some contacts in the field of Mesoamerican archaeology who might be able to help. I'll reach out to them and see if they've come across anything similar."

"Great," Ryan replied, clapping Ethan on the shoulder. "In the meantime, Sof and I can do some research on laser engraving equipment."

As they prepared to leave the alley, Sofia took one last look at the calavera, her mind racing with possibilities. The killer had left behind a puzzle, and she was determined to solve it—not only for the sake of justice, but for the memory of the victim whose life had been so cruelly cut short.

The oppressive weight of the mystery settled heavily on her shoulders as they stepped out of the alley and into the vibrant chaos of the Día de los Muertos celebration. The colors seemed more muted now, the laughter tinged with a haunting echo. Even as Sofia marveled at the beauty of the festival, she was plagued by a sense of foreboding.

Ryan was watching her. "Hey," he said, his eyes soft with concern. "You alright?"

"I just keep thinking about that calavera," she said.

"Trying to figure out what it's supposed to mean?"

"That's just it. I don't know what those symbols mean exactly, but I think I get the gist of the skull."

He studied her, puzzled. "Go on."

"It's a warning, Ryan. Whoever left it..." She paused as the weight of the unspoken thought settled in. "They want us to know they're not done yet."

CHAPTER FOUR

"Why would he leave the calavera on one victim, but not the other?" Sofia mused.

They were standing outside LaserCraft Creations, staring at the glass storefront that reflected the afternoon sun like a beacon. The November breeze carried the faint scent of ocean salt as it ruffled her hair, momentarily distracting her from the mystery that consumed her thoughts. The street was lined with an eclectic mix of shops and cafés, each adding its own unique flavor to the Californian landscape.

"That's a great question," Ryan said.

Sofia gave him a sidelong glance. "Which means you don't have any theories."

He shrugged one shoulder. "Not yet. Right now, I'm just trying to figure out what that damn skull is about."

"Well, then, what are we waiting out here for?"

Sofia pushed open the door of the engraver store and entered.

Inside, the air was filled with the distinct smell of burnt wood and metal. Shelves upon shelves of engraved items adorned the walls, ranging from intricate jewelry to personalized flasks. A large counter separated the store into two sections, dividing the customer area from where the engraving magic happened.

Sofia watched the owner, a middle-aged man with glasses perched on the tip of his nose, as he talked with a customer. The two of them spoke animatedly about the process of engraving a custom design onto a stainless-steel pocket watch. The customer, an older gentleman with a bushy mustache, seemed excited about the prospect of having such a unique keepsake.

"Imagine how fantastic it'll look when it's finished!" he exclaimed, clutching the pocket watch in his hand.

"Absolutely," the owner agreed, smiling warmly. "We pride ourselves on our precision and attention to detail. I assure you, your design will come to life."

As Sofia and Ryan wandered past them, Sofia couldn't help but overhear the conversation. Her mind, however, was still preoccupied with the calavera and the possible connection to the laser engraving process. She couldn't shake the feeling that understanding this aspect of the mystery would be a significant breakthrough in their case.

The owner finally wrapped up his conversation, pocketing the cash from the satisfied customer and waving him off with a cheerful farewell. He then turned his attention to Sofia and Ryan, his inquisitive eyes scanning over them as if trying to determine their intentions. With a neatly trimmed beard and hair slicked back, he exuded confidence and professionalism.

"Good afternoon," he said, adjusting his glasses. "How may I assist you today?"

"We're hoping you can help us identify a specific type of laser engraving," Sofia said. "We have this picture of some symbols." She pulled out her phone, showing the image of the calavera's engraved markings. The owner leaned in, examining the picture closely.

"Interesting," he mused, running a hand through his hair. "I must admit I've never seen anything quite like it. Unfortunately, I can't really pinpoint a specific laser based on just these symbols."

Sofia bit her lip, contemplating her next move. "Could we perhaps try some sample engravings with your different lasers?" she suggested. "Maybe we can find a match that way."

The owner hesitated, glancing at the machinery behind the counter. "I'm not sure about that," he replied reluctantly. "You see, using the equipment for non-business purposes could void their warranty, and the machines are rather expensive."

Sofia exchanged a glance with Ryan, who stepped in to offer support. "We understand that, but this is crucial information for an ongoing investigation. We promise to be careful, and we'll take full responsibility if anything happens."

The owner raised an eyebrow, clearly weighing the pros and cons. Sensing his hesitation, Sofia decided to appeal to his curiosity. "This might be a unique opportunity to learn more about the capabilities of your lasers, don't you think? Besides, we'll be sure to recommend your store to others if you can help us."

Finally, the owner relented with a sigh. "Alright," he agreed, "but you both have to follow my instructions closely. These machines are not toys, and I won't tolerate any negligence."

"Of course," Sofia assured him, a hint of excitement in her voice as they prepared to delve deeper into the enigma of the calavera's markings.

The owner led Sofia and Ryan through a narrow corridor, past shelves filled with delicate glassware and metal trinkets, into the heart of his workshop. The scent of burnt wood and hot metal grew stronger, an ode to the countless hours spent perfecting his craft.

"Here," he said, handing them each a pair of safety glasses. "You'll need these."

Sofia slipped the glasses on, momentarily distracted by the distorted world they presented. Ryan followed suit, casting her a reassuring glance as they stepped further into the room.

The owner gestured toward two machines, one significantly larger than the other. "These are my diode and CO_2 lasers," he explained, his voice tinged with pride. "I use them for most of my engravings."

"Could you please perform some sample engravings with these?" Sofia asked, holding out the photograph of the calavera's markings. "We're trying to find a match."

With a sigh of acquiescence, the owner fired up the machines, the hum of the lasers filling the room. He deftly maneuvered the controls, creating a series of intricate designs on small wooden plaques. However, despite his best efforts, none of the engravings seemed to resemble the symbols in the photograph.

"See? I told you it wouldn't be that simple," he grumbled, wiping sweat from his brow. "I think we've done enough here."

But Sofia wasn't ready to give up just yet. As the owner moved to shut down the machines, her gaze flickered to a dusty corner where a smaller laser sat, clearly neglected. A hunch told her that there was something special about this machine, something worth investigating.

"Wait," she said. "What about that one over there?"

The owner frowned, following her line of sight. "That old thing?" he scoffed. "It's an outdated model, hardly ever used. I doubt it would be of any use to you."

"Please. We've come this far, and we need to explore every possibility. Just one more sample engraving."

Reluctantly, the owner agreed, muttering under his breath as he prepared the forgotten machine. The laser whirred to life, its once-dormant light flickering like a ghostly apparition.

As the final design took shape, Sofia's heart caught in her throat. There, on the small wooden plaque, was a near-perfect replica of the calavera's markings: the same loops and curls, the same depth and width.

Sofia looked from the engraving to Ryan, excitement coursing through her veins. "We've found it," she said, barely able to contain her exhilaration. "No question it's the same."

The owner seemed surprised by their success but said nothing, his eyes locked on the uncanny similarity between the two engravings. For a moment, they all stood in thoughtful silence.

Ryan turned to the owner, his brow furrowed in curiosity. "So, what can you tell us about this laser?"

The owner appeared hesitant but eventually answered. "It's a rare brand," he admitted, his tone tinged with a mixture of pride and unease. "Enertronix Tech—unusual name, I know. Not many engraving shops have one of these anymore. But I assure you that my laser was not used to engrave your calavera. I'd remember, and I'm the only one who has access to these machines."

Sofia nodded, her gaze unwavering as she scrutinized the man. She could sense his sincerity, and she had no reason to doubt him. It still wouldn't hurt to check him out later, though. She made a mental note to run a background check on him, just in case.

With a grateful smile, she extended her hand. "Thank you for your help," she said warmly. "This has been invaluable."

"Of course," he replied, shaking her hand. "I hope you find what you're looking for."

As they left the store, the afternoon sunlight washed over them, casting elongated shadows on the pavement. The air was crisp, carrying a faint scent of autumn leaves and impending rain. Sofia's thoughts raced, her mind working to piece together the puzzle before them.

Pulling out her phone, she looked up the number for Enertronix Tech, then called it. A woman's voice answered, her tone guarded and slightly impatient.

"This is Special Agent Sofia Blake with the FBI," Sofia began, her voice calm and authoritative. "I need some information on your laser engravers. It's crucial to an ongoing investigation."

"FBI?" the woman repeated, sounding a touch uncertain. "What's this about?"

"I can't go into detail on an active investigation, but we believe that one of your lasers might have been used in a crime. Can you provide me with a list of clients who have purchased your laser engraver?"

The woman hesitated. "I'm sorry, I'm really not sure I'm the person you should be speaking with."

Sofia sighed, trying not to lose her patience. The woman was just doing her job, after all.

"Alright," she said. "Can I speak with your supervisor, then?"

"He's out of town at the moment, but I can give you his number." She laughed nervously. "He won't be thrilled getting a work-related call while he's sailing, I'm sure, but he'll understand when he learns it's the FBI."

Sofia considered this idea for a moment, then dismissed it. There was no telling whether this supervisor would even answer the phone, especially if he was on a boat, and even if he *did* answer, he might not want to give Sofia the information she needed. The last thing she wanted to do was get bogged down in red tape, forcing her to get a warrant to access the company's records.

"What's your name?" she asked.

The woman sounded surprised. "Barbara. But I go by Barb."

"Okay, Barb. I know I said I can't share details about this investigation, but I will share one: This is a *homicide* investigation. It's possible this has nothing to do with your company, but I won't know until I have that customer list."

Barbara got quiet. "I could really get in a lot of trouble for doing this."

"And more lives could be lost if you don't."

There was a long pause. Then the woman sighed. "Oh, what the heck," she said. "Just give me a minute."

"Thank you," Sofia said, relief flooding her.

A moment later, the woman was back on the line. "It's not much of a list—we discontinued the product shortly after it was released due to overheating issues."

"That's fine," Sofia said, thinking it was even better if they didn't have a long list of names to eliminate. "How many names are on that list? I'm specifically looking for anyone in the San Francisco area. Say, within two or three hundred miles of the city."

There was a long pause.

"Still there?" Sofia asked.

"Yeah," Barbara replied, a frown in her voice. She tapped a few keys. "Looks like I've got five in the San Francisco area who still have their devices. The rest returned theirs."

Sofia's heartbeat went up a notch. "Can you give me those five names, please?" She put the phone on speaker, and as Barbara read off the names, Ryan typed them into his own phone.

"Thank you," Sofia said to Barbara. "I really can't tell you how much this means."

"Don't mention it," Barbara said lightly, sounding at peace with her decision. "When you said you were with the FBI and you started asking about those machines, I thought maybe they'd overheated and killed someone. Good luck finding whoever you're after."

Sofia hung up the phone and pocketed it, her gaze locked on Ryan as he furiously tapped away at the screen of his own device.

"Got something?" she asked.

"Two of these people have criminal records," Ryan muttered, his fingers flying over the touchscreen as he accessed the police database. He glanced up at Sofia, his eyes filled with determination. "One of them is currently out of town, but the other... He lives nearby."

"Who is he?" Sofia's breath hitched in anticipation, her fingers curling into fists at her sides.

"Name's Hector Mendoza," Ryan replied. "His rap sheet's a mile long—assault, drug possession, attempted murder."

Sofia nodded, her heart pounding. "Sounds like we should pay him a visit."

CHAPTER FIVE

Santo sat on a rickety wooden chair, positioned just far enough from the main thoroughfare to avoid the pressing throngs of people. He watched as they moved through the festival, their faces painted in garish mockeries of grinning skulls, their clothing adorned with marigolds and sugar skull designs.

From his vantage point, he could see the many stalls that lined the streets: vendors selling pan de muerto, candied fruits, and intricate sugar skulls, artists offering to paint faces or sketch portraits, children darting between the stands, laughing as they chased after one another. It was a scene of joy, a celebration of life in the face of death.

Yet Santo could not help but feel that these people were missing something crucial. He had his own way of honoring the dead, a secret ritual known only to him.

As he observed the revelers, Santo found himself imagining the lives they led when they weren't parading around in skeleton makeup. The young couple sharing a plate of churros, no doubt caught up in the throes of a shallow, fleeting romance. The old man sitting alone on a nearby bench, his gnarled hands clutching a photograph of his deceased wife—surely, he must be filled with regret for the years squandered on petty arguments and unfulfilled dreams. And the family gathered around an elaborate ofrenda, lighting candles, and laying out offerings for their departed loved ones—what sort of secrets did they harbor behind their closed doors?

Such pretenders, Santo thought with a sneer, his disdain growing as he continued to watch the seemingly carefree festivalgoers. They danced and sang, gorged themselves on sweet treats, and posed for photographs with their painted faces, all the while believing they were paying tribute to the dead. But Santo knew better. True reverence for those who had passed on required a much deeper understanding of death, and a willingness to embrace its darker aspects.

None of them could ever comprehend the depths of my devotion, he mused silently, his gaze sweeping over the sea of painted skulls and festive decorations. *They are mere children playing a game, not true believers in the power of the dead.* He shifted in his chair, the weight of his secret knowledge pressing down upon him.

A cacophony of laughter assaulted his ears, drawing his attention to an approaching group of teenagers. Their faces were painted in garish imitation of calaveras, their voices loud and grating as they exchanged crude jokes among themselves. Santo could feel his anger building inside with each step the teenagers took toward him, their mirthful ignorance mocking the solemnity of the occasion.

"Can you believe she actually wore that?" one girl giggled, pointing at a nearby reveler. "It's like she has no idea what this is all about!"

"Right?" replied another, rolling her eyes. "Some people just don't get it."

None of you do, Santo thought bitterly, clenching his fists tightly. The hypocrisy of these children, so blind to their own shallowness, was unbearable. He could not sit idly by any longer, allowing them to profane the sacred day with their empty words and even emptier minds.

As the teenagers got closer, Santo decided he couldn't take it anymore. Gripping the edges of his chair with white-knuckled fury, he rose abruptly and walked off down the street, trying to calm himself. The echo of their laughter seemed to follow him, taunting him as he attempted to distance himself from the source of his ire.

His breathing heavy and labored, Santo reached into his pocket and withdrew a handful of knuckle bones. To him, they were much more than mere trinkets—they were relics of the dead, imbued with the essence of those who had once lived and breathed. As he shook them in his hand, their rhythmic clatter served as a reminder of the true nature of death: dark, inevitable, and filled with secrets beyond the comprehension of most.

"Focus," he told himself, his thoughts racing like a runaway train. "You cannot allow their ignorance to distract you from your purpose." The knuckle bones rattled in his hand, their sound drowning out the fading laughter of the teenagers. Santo felt a sense of calm slowly envelop him, as if the bones had absorbed his anger like a sponge, leaving behind only the cold certainty of his convictions.

He closed his eyes, allowing the rhythmic clatter of the knuckle bones to guide his steps. His anger had not yet fully subsided but the meditation he had learned across countless years was helping him regain control. He imagined his thoughts as ripples in a pond, slowly settling until it was still once more.

"Watch it!" a gruff voice snapped, jolting Santo from his meditation. Someone bumped into him, their shoulder colliding with his arm, and one of the knuckles flew from his hand. He watched it bounce along the street before coming to a stop, pointing at a young woman.

She stood there, her hair cascading like a waterfall of dark chocolate curls over her shoulders. An intricate sugar skull mask obscured half of her face, drawing attention to her piercing emerald eyes. Her red lace-edged dress clung to her slim figure, swaying gently as she moved with a fluid grace that seemed almost ethereal.

"Watch where you're going next time," the man who had collided with Santo muttered before stalking away, leaving the scent of cheap cologne lingering in his wake.

Santo barely registered the words, his gaze fixed upon the young woman who remained oblivious to the bone at her feet. Her eyes were distant, as if she too sensed the superficiality of the festival's revelry around them. Perhaps, Santo mused, she understood the true nature of the celebration—the honoring of those who had crossed the veil between life and death.

As the young woman started to walk away, Santo went over to the bone and picked it up. He stared after her, the feeling of destiny binding them together like an invisible thread tugging at his soul. She had been chosen by fate, or perhaps by the spirits of the dead themselves.

The knuckle bones remained in his hand as he followed her, their weight serving as a reminder of the task that lay before him. He would not fail them—those who had come before, and who now whispered to him from beyond the grave. Their voices swirled around him, urging him forward, drawing him ever closer to the young woman whose life was about to become irrevocably entwined with his own.

"Tonight," he promised the spirits, "justice will be served."

And with each step, he felt the shadows of the dead converge around him, their cold embrace both a comfort and a warning.

31

CHAPTER SIX

"This isn't where I'd expect someone like Hector Mendoza to be living," Sofia said as she piloted the Charger down the tree-lined street.

Palm Hideaway was a beautiful, gated community set high in the California hills. The lawns were elegantly manicured, and the grandiose mansions seemed to shimmer with wealth and privilege.

"Appearances can be deceiving," Ryan said, staring out the window as he studied the houses.

Sofia knew he was right. Still, it was odd to think that someone with such a checkered past – someone who had spent so much of his life behind bars – would live in such a ritzy neighborhood.

Number 1204 finally came into view, and Sofia guided the Charger into the driveway. The house was a stately two-story colonial, its white facade gleaming in the afternoon sun. Wrought-iron fencing surrounded the property, and a stone walkway led to the dark wooden front door.

"No other vehicles," Sofia remarked as she unbuckled her seat belt. "Hope that doesn't mean he's not home."

"Probably just keeps his vehicle in the garage," Ryan said.

Sofia hoped he was right. She climbed out of the car and followed the stone walkway to the front door. She gave the door several firm raps, then cocked her head, listening closely for any signs of life within. When no answer came, she glanced at Ryan, who shrugged helplessly.

Sofia's gaze shifted to a nearby window, where she thought she saw movement—the briefest flicker of a shadow.

"Did you see that?" she whispered to Ryan, keeping her voice low. He nodded, his expression tense.

"Stay here," she said, walking cautiously toward the window. Her heartbeat quickened as she considered the possibility that Hector Mendoza might be inside, watching them.

Just as she got close to the window, the curtains rustled and suddenly the fluffy face of a Pomeranian emerged, all teeth as it barked ferociously at her. The sudden appearance of the dog made her jump, and she let out an involuntary gasp.

"Looks like you made a friend," Ryan said, chuckling.

"Easy, little guy," Sofia murmured, trying to calm both the dog and her own racing pulse. Its angry yaps continued, muffled by the glass.

Just then the door creaked open, revealing a middle-aged woman with damp tendrils of dark hair clinging to her forehead and neck. She wore a faded floral bathrobe, hastily tied at the waist, and her eyes were guarded, questioning.

"Who are you? What do you want?" Her voice was tight, almost suspicious.

Sofia took a step forward, raising her badge as she introduced herself and Ryan. "I'm Special Agent Sofia Blake, and this is my partner, Special Agent Ryan Donovan. We're with the FBI. Are you Hector Mendoza's mother?"

The woman hesitated, her gaze flickering between the two agents, but finally nodded. "Catalina. But if you came here to take my son away or accuse him of something, you can leave right now." She kept the door mostly closed, her body tense as she peered at them through the narrow gap. Her wary eyes seemed to be searching for any signs of deception or ill intent on their faces.

Meanwhile, the barking Pomeranian continued its frenzied attempts to protect its mistress, sniffing at her feet as it tried to push past her to confront the strangers outside.

"Ma'am, we're not here to cause trouble," Sofia assured her gently, trying to ease the tension in the air. "We just have a few questions about a laser engraving machine your son may have purchased. Can we come in and talk?"

Catalina hesitated, saying nothing. As she waited for Catalina's response, Sofia found herself acutely aware of the subtle sounds around her—the hum of bees flitting between nearby flowers, the distant laughter of children playing in a neighboring yard, and beneath it all, the steady tick-tock of her own heartbeat. The late afternoon sun cast long shadows over the manicured lawn, painting everything in warm, golden hues that contrasted starkly with the nature of the issue that had brought them there.

"Look, we don't want to cause any trouble," she added. "We're simply investigating some laser engraving machines and want to talk to your son about his."

Catalina hesitated, her gaze shifting between Sofia and Ryan as if weighing their intentions. Finally, with a heavy sigh, she relented. "Alright, come in. But please, be quick about it." She bent down and grabbed the dog by the collar, preventing it from lunging at them as they crossed the threshold.

"Thank you," Sofia murmured, stepping into the house as the woman led the Pomeranian away, its barks sharp in the hallway. As

Catalina secured the dog behind a closed door, Sofia took a moment to study her surroundings.

The living room was modestly furnished, with an overstuffed sofa and a well-worn armchair facing an outdated television set. Family photos adorned the walls, capturing happier times of Hector and his mother—trips to the beach, birthday celebrations, graduations. The scent of lingering cigarette smoke clung to the air, mingling with the faint aroma of home-cooked meals long since enjoyed.

It was clear that Hector and his mother were the only two residents, their lives intertwined and displayed throughout the home. The care and love evident in each photograph spoke of a bond that had withstood the test of time and hardship, leaving Sofia with a pang of sympathy for the woman who had fought so hard to protect her son.

As Sofia continued to take in the details, she couldn't help but think about the complexity of Hector's life. On one hand, he was a man with a checkered past, someone who had undoubtedly made mistakes. But on the other hand, he was also a son, tethered to a woman who would do anything to safeguard him from harm.

"Does Hector still have the laser engraver?" Sofia prompted gently, breaking the silence as Catalina returned to the living room.

She nodded. "Yes, he still has it. But I swear he hasn't done anything wrong."

"Would you mind letting us see it?" Ryan asked.

Catalina hesitated. Then, as if realizing there was no point in balking now that she had already let them into the house, she nodded.

Sofia and Ryan followed the woman down a narrow hallway adorned with more family photos, then stopped at a closed door. The room inside was cramped, but neat, dominated by a desk in the center upon which sat the laser engraver.

"Here it is," Catalina said, gesturing to the machine. "But I don't know if Hector's been using it or not."

"What did he buy it for?" Ryan asked.

Catalina hesitated. "Some kind of business idea, I think. It didn't work out very well, as I recall."

"Thank you, Catalina," Sofia replied, her eyes scanning the room for any sign of recent activity. "And we understand your concerns. We're not here to make things difficult for you or your son."

The tension in Catalina's shoulders eased slightly as she let out a small sigh. "I'm sorry for being so suspicious," she admitted. "It's just...Hector's had a rough time with the police in the past, so I can't help but be protective."

Sofia studied a photograph on the desk, one that showcased a younger Hector with his arm around a beaming Catalina. It was a moment of genuine happiness, captured and preserved within the frame.

"You really love your son," she observed softly, touched by the affection between them.

"More than anything," Catalina whispered, her voice thick with emotion.

"Where is Hector right now?" Sofia asked gently, unwilling to push too hard, but needing the answer all the same.

Catalina hesitated, her eyes darting away for a brief moment. It was then that Ryan stepped in, his tone matter of fact yet empathetic. "Catalina, we're investigating a pair of homicides. We don't know if Hector is involved or not, but we need to talk to him to find out."

Shock rippled across Catalina's face, her hands trembling ever so slightly. "No, you must be mistaken," she stammered. "Hector wouldn't...he couldn't..."

"Please, Catalina," Sofia pleaded, her heart aching for the woman who was torn between loyalty and fear. "We just need to speak to him."

Catalina sighed, her eyes filling with tears as she resigned herself to the truth. "He works at a store called 'Townsend's Hardware.' It's on Main Street, just a few blocks from here. You can't miss it."

"Thank you, Catalina," Sofia said, touched by the woman's vulnerability. Ryan nodded, his expression softening as he regarded the distressed mother.

As they turned to leave, Catalina reached out, her voice cracking under the weight of her emotions. "Hector might have made some mistakes, but he's not a bad person. He had a difficult upbringing; I wasn't able to provide him with the life he needed." She paused, wiping away a stray tear that threatened to spill down her cheek. "Please, don't judge him too harshly."

Sofia offered Catalina a reassuring smile, one filled with empathy and understanding. "We'll do our best to help him, I promise." With that, she and Ryan made their way back to the car, leaving behind a mother who was both hopeful and fearful for her son's future.

As they settled into the vehicle, Sofia couldn't shake the image of Catalina's tear-streaked face from her mind. Was Hector innocent, or was it possible that Catalina had raised a monster without even knowing it?

* * *

The store was a sprawling, single-story building with a faded blue façade, a relic from a bygone era of mom-and-pop businesses struggling to survive in a world increasingly dominated by corporate chains.

"Charming little place," Ryan said.

Sofia nodded. "Looks like it's fallen on hard times, though, given the fact that we're the only ones here."

As Sofia surveyed the empty parking lot, she felt a flicker of unease as she imagined that Catalina might have lied to them about Hector's whereabouts. Then it occurred to her that the more likely explanation was just that Catalina had dropped Hector off. He might even have walked, given how close the store was to his house.

As Sofia and Ryan stepped through the front doors of the hardware store, a bell tinkled overhead, announcing their arrival. Inside, the air was heavy with the scent of sawdust, paint, and metal. The walls were lined with shelves stocked meticulously with an array of tools and supplies, while the floor was a labyrinth of aisles waiting to be explored.

"Hello?" Sofia called out tentatively, her voice loud in the empty store. There was no reply, only the distant hum of fluorescent lights overhead.

"Let's split up and search for him," Ryan suggested, his eyes scanning the deserted aisles. "I'll take the left side; you take the right."

"Got it." Sofia nodded, her pulse quickening with anticipation as she ventured deeper into the store.

As she wound her way through the maze of merchandise, Sofia couldn't help but feel a sense of unease creeping over her. The silence was oppressive, broken only by the occasional creak of a floorboard underfoot. Every shadow seemed to hold a secret.

Suddenly, a door at the back of the store swung open with a low groan, and a man stepped out into the dim light. His dark hair was plastered to his forehead, beads of sweat glistening on his brow. He wore a stained apron over his work clothes, a clear indication that he was an employee. But it was the bruises mottling his face – the angry purples and yellows of recent violence – that caught Sofia's attention.

"Hector Mendoza?" Ryan called out.

The man's eyes widened in shock and fear. For a moment he just stood there, paralyzed.

Take it easy, Sofia thought as she moved toward him. *Don't make this more complicated than it has to–*

But before she could finish the thought, the man spun on his heels and darted back through the door he'd just emerged from.

CHAPTER SEVEN

Sofia's heart raced as she and Ryan chased Hector Mendoza into the back of the hardware store.

The room was dimly lit, casting eerie shadows on the cluttered shelves that lined the walls. It smelled of sawdust and oil, creating a thick atmosphere that made it hard to breathe. Piles of paint cans, hammers, and various tools littered the floor, making it difficult to move quickly without tripping.

Sofia saw a door at the end of the room, one that presumably led outside. She was heading toward it when her ears picked up a strange sound she couldn't quite identify. She slowed, listening.

"Come on!" Ryan said as he rushed past her.

Sofia scanned the room, suspicious that Hector might be hiding nearby. That was when she noticed a small gap between two shelves. Peering into the darkness, she discovered a flight of stairs leading down. Faint voices rose from below, punctuated by the occasional yell or cheer.

"Wait!" she shouted.

Ryan hit the exterior door and threw it open, filling the room with the afternoon sunlight. Then he turned back, impatient.

"What are you waiting for?" he demanded.

Sofia pointed at the flight of stairs. Ryan cocked his head, his eyes widening as he registered the sounds emanating from the hidden basement.

"What is that?" he asked.

Sofia shook her head. "No idea. Let's go find out."

The voices grew louder as Sofia and Ryan descended the stairs, and the atmosphere changed. At the bottom of the stairs, Sofia entered what appeared to be an underground boxing club. Bare concrete walls were illuminated by a few dim, flickering lights hanging from the ceiling, casting shadows on the crowd that surrounded a makeshift ring in the center.

Sofia's eyes locked onto the two men in the ring engaged in a brutal bare-knuckle fight. Their faces were bloodied, and their fists moved with lightning speed, landing bone-crunching punches on each other.

The spectators around them shouted and cheered, urging their preferred fighter on.

"Can you believe this place?" Ryan muttered under his breath. But Sofia was barely listening; her eyes scanned the room, searching for Hector Mendoza.

And there he was, standing at the back of the room, staring warily at them as he spoke to a squat, bald man.

Sofia nudged Ryan and pointed toward Hector. "There he is," she whispered. "Let's go."

They pushed through the crowd, but before they could reach Hector, the bald man stepped in their way. He had clearly been in numerous fights—his face was a map of scars, and his cauliflower ears attested to a long history of violence. Every inch of him looked as solid as brick.

"Where do you think you're going?" he growled, his voice gravelly and menacing.

"We need to talk to Hector Mendoza,' Sofia replied, trying her best to maintain her composure.

"Piss off," the scarred man said.

"We're federal agents," Ryan said, not backing down. "Which means you're interfering with a federal investigation."

"Why don't you get to the part where I give a damn?"

"I bet you'll give a damn when I'm leading you out in cuffs."

The scarred man's lips curled into a sinister grin, and he leaned in closer to Ryan, his breath hot and reeking of stale tobacco. "You try that, pretty boy, and you'll be leaving here in a body bag."

Sofia's heart raced as she considered potential strategies. She could call for backup, alert the local police about this illegal fighting ring, but there was a good chance Hector would use the ensuing chaos to slip away unnoticed. They needed another option, something that wouldn't risk losing their suspect.

But what could they do?

The crowd around them pressed closer, their stares hostile. Sofia looked back toward the stairs and saw there was now a wall of bodies.

"You see," the scarred man said, "we've got a little problem here. If we let you go, the first thing you're going to do is rat on us, and we can't have that. It's just not good for business."

Sofia swallowed hard, watching the figures around her to see who would make the first move. "So you're going to kill us, is that it?" she asked. "If you think you'll be in hot water for participating in a few illegal fights, just imagine what's going to happen if you harm us."

The man's eyes twinkled. "That's assuming anyone finds out what happened. You two could just...disappear. Never heard from again." He dusted his hands.

The figures pressed closer. Several of them had prison tattoos Sofia recognized, and she wondered how many of them might be violating their parole by being here. She and Ryan were a threat to these men just by showing up, and it seemed they could no longer just walk away.

Someone stepped forward and gave Ryan a shove. Ryan shoved the man back.

"Back off!" Ryan growled, drawing his weapon. Sofia did the same, turning and putting her back to Ryan's. "We're not going to be the only ones leaving here in body bags!" he said.

The scarred man chuckled. "You know how long some of us have been waiting to get our hands on someone like you?"

Sofia looked at Hector, who was watching them intently. "Is this what you want?" she asked. "This won't just be the end of your shady little side-business--your life will be over, too. Think of your mother."

Hector blinked at her, saying nothing.

The scarred man pulled out a knife and snapped it open. He grinned. "Well, boys, they can't shoot us all at once, can they?"

Several of the men close to Sofia tensed, ready to spring. She slipped her finger to the trigger.

Just then, Hector spoke up. "Wait a minute!" he said. "I might have a...how do you say...*compromiso*?"

Sofia nodded, still watching the men around her. "We're listening."

"You want to take me away? Then your friend there fights me. He wins, I go. I win, *you* go."

"They'll just come back with more agents," the scarred man growled.

"Not if they leave everything," Hector added. "Guns, badges, handcuffs, *todo*."

"Deal," Ryan said, lowering his weapon.

Sofia's head jerked toward her partner. "Ryan, are you serious?"

He holstered his weapon. "You see a better way out of this?"

"No, but—" She shook her head, unable to believe what was happening. "I know you can hold your own, but he's a trained fighter. He does this for a living."

"Which will make it that much sweeter when I knock him on his ass," Ryan said.

Sofia's stomach did a somersault as she watched Ryan unbutton his shirt and pull it over his head. He was in good shape, his body toned

40

and muscular, but even so, he was much slimmer than Hector. And even though Sofia knew Ryan had taken martial arts training beyond what was required by the Bureau, she wasn't sure whether he'd ever gone up against someone as experienced as Hector.

"Are you sure about this?" she asked, touching Ryan's arm. "We don't know what he's capable of."

"That goes both ways, sister," Ryan said, his blue eyes filled with determination.

CHAPTER EIGHT

As Ryan stepped into the makeshift ring, Sofia felt a gnawing worry lodge itself in her chest. This was not how she had envisioned their pursuit of Hector Mendoza going.

The more she thought about it, though, the less she was surprised that Ryan had so willingly accepted the offer of a fight. Ryan had always been a risk taker—it was, he'd once told her, the only way he could survive the streets of New York City, where he'd walked the beat as a twenty-two-year-old, fresh out of the academy, following in the footsteps of his father who had been killed in the line of duty. That drive to take risks, no matter the personal cost, was what made him so good at his job.

And it was always what made Sofia worry he would get himself killed.

"Be careful," she whispered as Ryan prepared to face off against Hector, praying that they both would make it out of the underground club alive and with Hector as their captive.

Hector joined Ryan in the ring. The dim light above them flickered, casting eerie shadows on the fighters' faces. Sweat beaded on Ryan's brow, but his expression remained focused and determined.

"Ready to lose, gringo?" Hector asked, smirking at Ryan. The tension in the room was palpable as the crowd of spectators eagerly awaited the first move.

"Save your breath," Ryan replied coolly as he began to circle his opponent.

Hector struck first, landing a few solid punches on Ryan's torso. To Sofia's dismay, her partner seemed content to take the hits, offering little resistance. She clenched her fists, willing him to fight back, but he continued to bide his time, blocking, and dodging where he could.

The man with the scars sidled up to Sofia, a cruel grin etching itself across his weathered face. "Your partner doesn't stand a chance," he sneered, watching the fight unfold with sadistic glee.

"Ryan knows what he's doing," she muttered under her breath, refusing to give the brute the satisfaction of seeing her worry. Inwardly, though, she couldn't help but question whether Ryan had overestimated his abilities.

Just then, Ryan struck back. With a deft combination of jabs and hooks, he forced Hector to give ground. Soon the cheers of the crowd faded to an uneasy silence, replaced by the thud of fists connecting with flesh. The man with the scars glared at Sofia before stalking away in frustration.

Ryan continued to press his advantage, landing a series of punishing strikes against Hector's midsection and face. For every hit Hector blocked, Ryan found an opening and landed another punishing blow. The fight seemed to be turning in Ryan's favor—that is until Hector landed an unexpected uppercut that sent Ryan reeling backwards into the ropes.

Hector seized the opportunity, raining down a flurry of punches while Ryan desperately tried to defend himself.

"No, no, no," Sofia murmured. Her heart pounded in rhythm with each punch, her nerves tangled in knots. Furtively, she slipped her phone out and began texting a friend at Bureau headquarters, asking him to send backup. She hoped they wouldn't need it, but there was no telling what might happen.

Hector swung a haymaker at Ryan, a blow that might very well have knocked Ryan out cold--if it had connected. Instead, Ryan managed to duck the blow and throw a hard jab at Hector's chest that sent him staggering backwards across the ring. Taking advantage of his brief respite, Ryan rushed forward and landed a series of lightning-fast kicks that sent Hector toppling to the ground.

The crowd fell deathly silent as Ryan stood over Hector, triumphant. He had done it—he had beaten Hector Mendoza at his own game.

Breathing heavily, Ryan turned to Sofia with a triumphant grin. Sweat glistened on his skin, his chest heaving as he fought to steady his breath. The air was thick with tension, the spectators' silence almost palpable.

"Looks like we're going to need those cuffs, after all," he said.

"I'm not so sure about that," the scarred man said, and Sofia glanced over to see him surrounded by a knot of men with hard, angry faces. "Hector may have made a deal with you, but I didn't."

Before she could stop them, the men lunged forward and attacked Ryan. Ryan, still reeling from his fight with Hector, backpedaled as they advanced on him.

Wasting no time, Sofia pulled herself up into the ring. As one of the men closed in on Ryan, she grabbed him from behind, twisted his arm behind his back, and shoved him aside.

"This wasn't the deal!" she said.

"Screw your deal!" the scarred man replied.

Sofia sidled up next to Ryan, sidestepping Hector's prone body as he lay on the mat. Ryan nodded at her, swallowing hard.

"Hey, Sof," he said, managing a gutsy grin as their attackers closed in on them. "Nice to have a friend at the end of the world, eh?"

There were a few dozen men now, far too many for Sofia and Ryan to fight alone. She drew her gun, but the scarred man only laughed.

"You're gonna need a lot of bullets," he said, seemingly unfazed at the prospect of getting shot.

Just then, a loud voice echoed through the room: "STOP!"

Sofia turned to see a group of police officers rushing toward them, guns drawn. The attackers scattered at once, disappearing into the shadows like cockroaches in sunlight. Ryan and Sofia watched as the officers began handcuffing their assailants one by one.

"Calling for backup?" Ryan said tiredly. "That's not playing fair."

"Looks like I wasn't the only one making up the rules as I went along."

Out of the corner of her eye, Sofia saw Hector crawling off the edge of the mat, trying to get around the group of officers so he could sprint to the stairs.

"Where you going, Hector?" she asked. At the sound of her voice, two of the officers turned in their direction, then hurried over to box him in. Hector glared at Sofia and Ryan.

"Are you going to honor your word?" Ryan asked. "Or do you want another go?"

For a few moments, it looked as though Hector might very well attack again. Then his fatigue seemed to get the better of him, and his shoulders slumped. The two officers approached from behind and handcuffed him.

"Now," Ryan said to Sofia as he walked over to his discarded shirt, "let's go find out what information we just worked so hard to get."

CHAPTER NINE

The sterile smell of the police station interrogation room hung heavy in the air as Sofia walked in, clutching a pair of ice packs.

Let's hope Ryan's fight was worth it, she thought.

The small room, with its single flickering fluorescent light, seemed to buzz ominously. A cold metal table dominated the center, surrounded by bare white walls devoid of any decoration or warmth. It wasn't exactly a welcoming space, but it served its purpose.

Ryan sat across from Hector Mendoza, who was nursing a bruised jaw. In retrospect, Ryan's decision to fight Hector wasn't surprising— he liked to face life head-on, preferring the straightforward option whenever possible. Still, Sofia hadn't known he was quite so competent in the ring. It seemed he was still capable of surprising her, even after all these years.

He's reckless, she thought, feeling both troubled and full of admiration at the same time. *But somehow, his methods seem to pay off. Besides, how else were we going to get out of that situation without anyone getting killed? There was no other way we could have stalled until backup arrived.*

She handed an ice pack to Ryan and another to Hector, who accepted it grudgingly.

"Can we get you anything?" she asked as she took a seat, her eyes never leaving Hector's face. He shook his head, wincing slightly as he pressed the ice pack to his jaw.

"Let's start with the basics," she said. "Is your name Hector Mendoza?"

He nodded. "That is correct." It was clear that English wasn't his first language.

"¿Te sentirías más cómodo hablando en español?" Sofia asked in fluent Spanish. Hector looked up, surprise registering on his battered face. He nodded.

"Gracias, señorita," he said quietly, his dark eyes locked onto hers. Sofia knew well the importance of making a suspect feel at ease, especially when trying to uncover the truth.

Ryan's gaze flicked between Sofia and Hector before he leaned forward, his fingers laced together. "Ask him why he ran away from us," he said to Sofia, his voice low and stern.

"¿Por qué huiste de nosotros?" she inquired, relaying the question to Hector.

The bruised man hesitated, his eyes darting around the room as if searching for an escape. Finally, he spoke, his voice hoarse but steady. Sofia listened intently, nodding as she translated for Ryan.

"He thought we were there to bust the illegal boxing club he was hosting in the basement of his store," she said. "He says he was just trying to make some side money so he didn't have to keep depending on his mother, but he didn't want his mother to know about it."

Ryan's jaw tightened at the revelation, but his focus remained on Hector. "Ask him if he's ever been to La Porta," he said.

"¿Ha estado alguna vez en La Porta?" she asked Hector, watching the emotions play across his face as he processed the question.

"Si," he admitted, swallowing hard. *"He estado allí antes."*

Sofia turned to Ryan. "He *has* been there before," she confirmed. The air in the room grew colder, the tension thickening.

"What about the laser engraving machine at his house?" Ryan asked. "What did he get it for?"

"Cuéntame sobre la máquina de grabado láser que tienes en tu casa," she said to Hector. He replied, and again Sofia translated for Ryan.

"He bought it for his business, but it was never as useful as he thought it would be."

"What kind of business?" Ryan asked.

Hector hesitated for a moment, seeming to weigh his options before finally speaking.

"He was trying to start a custom jewelry store with a friend," Sofia translated. "He used the machine to engrave designs on his pieces. His friend bailed on the project, though, and they never really made any money. He hasn't used the engraver since then."

Sofia studied Hector's face, searching for any signs of deceit. The room seemed to grow smaller around them as the weight of their investigation pressed in. She decided it was time to see if Hector had an alibi for Jessenia Arjona's murder.

"¿Dónde estabas anoche?" she asked.

Hector's eyes flickered with uncertainty before he answered, *"Estaba peleando en mi club. Peleamos toda la noche."*

"He claims he was fighting in his club," Sofia said to Ryan. "They were up most of the night, fighting."

Ryan narrowed his eyes, a hint of skepticism lining his strong features. "Ask him if he has any evidence to back up that alibi."

"¿Tienes alguna prueba de que estabas allí anoche?" Sofia asked Hector.

"Y-yes," Hector stammered in broken English, beads of sweat forming on his brow as he glanced at Ryan. "I record fights, can access on phone." His eyes pleaded with Sofia's, desperation clear in their depths. "Please, my phone."

"Wait here," Ryan said, rising from the table and leaving the room. He had only been gone a few moments when Hector leaned toward Sofia, whispering.

"Por favor." He looked at Sofia, his dark eyes filled with a desperate plea. *"No le digas a mi madre sobre el club. Le rompería el corazón."*

Sofia met his gaze, noticing the vulnerability etched onto his face as he pleaded with her not to tell his mother about the illegal fight club. She empathized with his desire to protect his mother from the truth, and it tugged at her heartstrings.

"No tengo planes de decirle a tu madre, Hector," she reassured him gently. *"Pero necesitamos saber la verdad sobre anoche."*

"Gracias," he murmured, relief flooding his features as he leaned back.

Footsteps echoed in the hallway outside, and the door creaked open as Ryan re-entered the room. His broad-shouldered frame cast a shadow over them as he approached the table, Hector's phone in hand. "Here you go," he said, placing the device in front of Hector.

Hector unlocked the phone, then navigated to an app that appeared to be connected to a camera installed in his illegal boxing club. With bated breath, he opened a video and played it, pointing to the time signature in the corner.

"See?" Hector urged, his voice strained with urgency. "I am there, fighting."

Sofia couldn't help but notice the pleading in Hector's eyes as she reached out and carefully took the phone from him. Her fingers brushed against his calloused hands, a physical reminder of the rough life he had led. She held her breath, feeling the weight of the device in her grasp, and turned to Ryan.

"Let's take a closer look," she suggested, her heart pounding with anticipation. Together, they huddled over the small screen, their faces illuminated by the flickering images playing before them. The dim light cast eerie shadows in the cramped interrogation room, heightening the sense of dread that had settled within its walls.

As she fast-forwarded through the footage, Sofia watched the time signature increase steadily, minute by minute. Hector was indeed present in the basement throughout the course of the night, sweat glistening on his face as he threw punch after relentless punch. The sounds of fists connecting with flesh filled her ears, mingling with the raucous cheers of the crowd that surrounded the makeshift ring.

"Looks like he was there all night," Ryan muttered, his voice heavy with disappointment. "Seems we have no choice but to cut him loose."

As Ryan returned the phone to Hector and opened the door for him, ready to escort him out, Sofia thought of the crowds she had seen in La Porta celebrating the Day of the Dead. The killer was out there somewhere, perhaps using the festival to hide his identity.

And Sofia had a feeling he would be on the hunt again soon.

CHAPTER TEN

Santo followed the woman through the small town, his eyes – hidden beneath sunglasses – tracking her every movement.

She was a petite figure, her dark hair cascading down her back as she moved gracefully among the revelers. Santo could not help but notice the intensity in her eyes, a gaze that seemed to penetrate the very souls of those she passed.

Soon, he knew that he would be seeing those eyes much more closely. And they would not look so calm and self-possessed.

As Santo walked, he absentmindedly rattled the knuckle bones in his pocket, pondering the fate that had led him to this moment. It was a cruel reminder that everyone, even those who thought they were in control, were still at the mercy of some higher power.

The California sun cast long shadows across the cobblestone streets, illuminating the vibrant colors of the papel picado, which fluttered above the bustling crowd like spectral butterflies. The scent of marigolds and incense filled the air, while laughter and music echoed around Santo.

The woman turned to examine a rack of clothing being sold by a vendor, her fingers brushing over the embroidered fabric with a tenderness that betrayed her fascination.

"Beautiful, isn't it?" the vendor remarked, his voice rich with pride for his handiwork.

"Very," she replied, her voice soft yet assertive, the kind that demanded attention without ever needing to raise its volume.

Not wishing to be noticed if the woman should glance in his direction, Santo turned and feigned interest in a nearby display of sugar skulls. He kept watching her from the corners of his eyes, careful not to betray his intentions.

As the woman continued to peruse the garments before her, seemingly unaware of the danger lurking just a short distance away, Santo felt his resolve growing stronger. His heart pounded in his chest, the rhythmic beat serving as a constant reminder of the stakes at hand.

The woman resumed her stroll through the lively streets, and Santo followed suit. His fingers tightened around the knuckle bones as he weaved through the throng of people, their painted faces a macabre

49

blend of joy and sorrow. He tried to contain his impatience, but every person that stepped between him and his quarry seemed like an obstacle placed there by fate itself.

He muttered a curse under his breath as he brushed past a man carrying an armful of marigolds, their vibrant orange petals a stark contrast against the somber hues of the afternoon. The crowd thickened, and for a moment he lost sight of the woman.

Elbowing his way forward, Santo finally escaped the crowd and gained some breathing room. Then his heart sank.

Where had the woman gone?

His eyes darted back and forth, scanning the crowd for any sign of her. Panic began to bubble in his chest; each passing second felt like an eternity, and he cursed himself for letting her slip from his grasp. Had she spotted him? Was she gone for good?

Where are you? he thought, growing more desperate by the second.

Then, just as hope seemed lost, he caught a glimpse of her inside a nearby restaurant as she walked past the window. Her movements were graceful, almost ethereal, as if she were dancing to the beat of the mariachi band in the distance.

Santo hurried inside, grateful for the chance to continue his pursuit. The restaurant was dimly lit, with candles flickering atop rustic wooden tables. Rich aromas of spices and grilled meats filled the air, and the low murmur of conversation mingled with the clinking of glasses and silverware.

He scanned the room, his heart pounding in his ears as he searched for the woman. The light from the candles cast strange shadows on the faces of the patrons, transforming them into eerie visages that seemed to leer at him from the corners of his vision.

"Can I help you find a seat, señor?" asked a waiter who seemed to have materialized from nowhere. He smiled politely. The dim lighting danced on the man's face, casting shadows that seemed to accentuate his sunken cheeks.

"No, thank you," Santo said, his gaze darting across the room as he searched for the woman. "I'm meeting a friend."

"Very well." The waiter nodded before moving on to attend to other customers. As he disappeared into the sea of tables and patrons, Santo finally caught sight of the woman again. She was pushing through a doorway at the back of the room, and without hesitation, he followed.

The hallway he entered was more isolated than the bustling main area of the restaurant. Santo could hear the sounds of the kitchen coming through the wall—the sizzle of frying pans, the metallic clangs of pots and knives. It was a symphony of culinary chaos that only heightened his senses. His heart raced as beads of sweat formed on his brow, but he didn't see anyone else around.

As he continued down the corridor, the woman opened a door on the right side. Santo noticed her pausing for a moment, and their eyes locked. For a brief instant, time seemed to stand still, and he could feel the weight of her scrutiny like a physical presence. Was she onto him?

Damn it, he thought, his heart hammering against his ribs. *I should've been more careful.*

She turned away and continued through the doorway, leaving Santo with a mix of relief and unease.

Is she testing me, or just being cautious? he wondered, his mind racing with possibilities.

He moved down the hallway, his anticipation building with every step. When he reached the door, he hesitated for a fraction of a second before pushing it open.

The women's restroom smelled faintly of lavender and bleach, a stark contrast to the rich aromas that filled the restaurant outside. Fluorescent lights cast an eerie glow over the white tiles, making the room feel colder and more sterile than it should have been.

With cautious precision, Santo moved along the row of stalls, pressing his ear against each door as he went. He strained to hear any sound that might reveal the woman's presence—the rustle of fabric, a stifled breath, anything. His own breathing felt too loud, too conspicuous. He tried to silence it, focusing all his attention on the task at hand.

Is she hiding from me? Where could she have gone?

Then, when he was halfway down the row of stalls, the door at the end of the row opened with a soft creak and the woman stepped out, her gaze meeting Santo's reflection in the mirror. She stopped moving. Her eyes widened and she visibly stiffened, clearly unsettled by the sight of a man in the women's restroom.

"What are you doing here?" she demanded, her voice wavering only slightly.

Santo's heart pounded in his chest as he locked eyes with her. The air in the restroom seemed to crackle with tension, and for a moment, time seemed to stand still.

Then, without a word, Santo moved toward her with quick, decisive strides.

"Who are you?" she asked, the quiver in her voice more pronounced than before. She took a few steps back until she was bumping into the tiled wall.

Nowhere to run now, Santo thought.

Suddenly she snapped. "Stay away from me!" she shrieked, pressing herself against the wall. Her eyes darted frantically around the restroom, searching for an escape route. But there was nowhere to run—just the row of stalls behind her.

Desperate to escape his grasp, the woman retreated into one of the stalls, her hand shaking as she tried to slam the door shut. But Santo was too fast, catching the edge of it just before it could click into place. He could feel the force of her terror as she pushed against it, trying to keep him out. He was stronger than she was, however.

And he would not be denied.

With a guttural growl, Santo shoved the door open. The woman stumbled back, her eyes wide with horror as she pressed herself against the cold porcelain of the toilet. She looked like a cornered animal, her every muscle tensed and ready to spring.

"Please," she whimpered, her voice barely audible above the pounding of Santo's heart. "Just tell me what you—"

But that was all she managed to say before Santo grabbed her.

CHAPTER ELEVEN

So this is where the killer left his first victim, Sofia thought as she ducked beneath the caution tape and entered the partially renovated home.

The late afternoon California sun slanted through the grimy windows, casting long shadows across the dust-laden floor. Sofia glanced around, taking in the skeletal wooden framework that crisscrossed the once opulent room, the chandeliers now stripped of their crystal adornments and the peeling wallpaper revealing the crumbling plaster beneath.

"According to the police report," Ryan said, his voice seeming unnaturally loud in the abandoned space, "Roberta Lima was found right here in the middle of the room."

Sofia crouched down in the center, her dark eyes scanning the floor closely. Amid the sawdust and fine plaster dust from the ongoing renovations, she noticed a large area where the dust hadn't fallen as thickly, presumably where the victim had been lying. The discovery sent a chill down Sofia's spine, though she fought to keep her expression neutral.

Footprints in the dust were scattered haphazardly throughout the room, adding another layer to the macabre scene before her. Could they be the killer's? Or merely remnants of the crime scene investigators' movements?

"Did the report mention anything about these footprints?" she asked.

"Unfortunately, no," Ryan answered. "By the time police got here, the area had already been heavily disturbed. Apparently, a group of rowdy teenagers broke in here two nights ago, thinking to have a party, and instead stumbled upon Roberta Lima's body."

Sofia clenched her jaw at the thought of how the teenagers' carelessness might have cost them a valuable lead. She glanced around the room once more, trying to piece together any clues that might have been left behind.

As much as she wanted to believe there was some hidden significance to this location, she supposed the more likely explanation was that the killer had left Roberta's body here simply because this

53

house was safe from prying eyes. He'd left the other victim's body in an alley, after all—another location not easily seen by passersby.

Sofia's thoughts turned to the calavera that had been found on the second victim, Jessenia Arjona. Why hadn't the killer left a similar token with the first victim? Was there a reason for the discrepancy, or was it merely an oversight?

Her fingers brushed over the screen of her phone, bringing up the haunting image of the calavera left by the killer. The eerie symbols etched into the skull seemed to dance before her tired eyes, taunting her with their hidden meaning.

"Any progress?" Ryan asked.

"Nothing," she admitted, frustration creeping into her tone. "These symbols...they're like nothing I've ever seen."

The weight of failure pressed down on Sofia as she stared at the cryptic markings. It was as if a fog had settled around her thoughts, obscuring vital information just out of reach. She sighed heavily, rubbing her temples in an attempt to alleviate the mental strain.

"You'll figure it out," Ryan said. "Just a matter of time."

She nodded, appreciating his effort to encourage her even if it didn't help much.

Just then Ryan's phone rang. "It's the boss," he said to her as he took a few steps away. "Probably wants an update." He answered the phone and turned away from Sofia, facing the window.

Alone with her thoughts, Sofia wracked her brain for any semblance of a connection between the symbols and the case. She thought of Ethan Knight, the professor of Mesoamerican languages they'd met at the first crime scene. Maybe he'd have some thoughts on how to interpret the symbols.

The only problem was, she didn't have his number. She didn't know from where he'd graduated, either. In fact, she knew very little about the man--except, of course, that he was handsome, charming, and a skilled linguist.

She opened her phone and searched for his name in the browser. When she came across far too many results to sort through individually, she also added 'Mesoamerican' to the search. That did it. She found a scholarly article he'd written on Mayan hieroglyphics and, from that, she was able to track down where he'd received his degree. She quickly looked up the university's website and found a faculty directory. Sure enough, Ethan Knight's name popped up there with an email address and phone number listed.

"Gotcha," she murmured, calling the number.

The phone rang for a while before going to voicemail. Sofia was tempted to leave a message just so he'd have reason to call her back, but at the last moment she changed her mind. She found herself wanting to speak with him as much for personal reasons as for professional ones, and she couldn't have that kind of conflict right now.

Perhaps her parents could help her instead. Her father, Emilio, and her mother, Linette, were both renowned scholars, having spent their entire careers deciphering ancient texts and unraveling the mysteries of long-lost civilizations. Now retired, they continued to indulge their insatiable curiosity through personal research projects.

Sofia dialed the familiar number and waited for her father to answer. The phone rang once, twice, and then she heard his deep voice on the other end.

"Hello, Sofia," he said, a hint of amusement in his tone. "What brings my favorite FBI agent to calling today?"

"Hey, Dad," Sofia replied, fighting back the weariness that threatened to creep into her voice. Her father, Dr. Emilio Blake, had been a renowned archaeologist before transitioning to a part-time teaching role at a local university, a change that gave him more time to spend with his wife and take life at a slower pace. Sofia's relationship with her father was built on a foundation of mutual respect and friendly competition, each one pushing the other to achieve greatness. He never failed to remind her of her potential, even as he teased her about surpassing him one day.

"What's the occasion?" Emilio asked, his voice filled with warmth. "Did you miss the sound of my voice?"

Sofia smiled. "Actually, I'm working on this case and thought you might be able to help."

"Well, that hurts my feelings, but go ahead anyway."

"I'm working a double homicide, and the killer left a calavera – a sugar skull – on one of the victims. The skull has these strange symbols on it, but I can't seem to decipher them."

"Ah, a mystery!" Emilio exclaimed, his enthusiasm palpable even through the phone. "Tell me more about these symbols."

As Sofia described the markings on the calavera, she could hear her father's pen scratching furiously against paper, undoubtedly sketching out the symbols as she spoke. She took a deep breath, inhaling the lingering scent of sawdust and plaster, and tried to focus on the task at hand.

"Interesting," Emilio mused when she finished. "I have a few theories, but I'll need to do some research to see if any of them hold water. Have you considered the possibility that it might be a combination of different writing systems? Perhaps the killer was trying to obfuscate their message by using multiple languages."

Sofia frowned, considering his suggestion. "I suppose it's possible," she admitted slowly. "Some of the symbols appear to incorporate elements of Nahuatl, but then others don't seem to match any language I'm familiar with. And as you know, that's quite a few."

"Indeed, my polyglot daughter." Emilio chuckled. "I think—" He paused, and Sofia heard a voice in the background. Emilio sighed theatrically. "It seems I must share you with your mother. Hold on."

As Emilio handed the phone over, Sofia could hear her mother's voice in the background, playfully scolding him for hogging the conversation.

"Hi, sweetie," Linette Blake said warmly. "I heard you two talking about the calavera, and I couldn't help but wonder if there might be any cultural significance to the symbols. Have you looked into that?"

Sofia smiled at the sound of her mother's voice, always so full of curiosity and warmth. Linette had been an anthropologist before she retired and was now writing books about the various cultures she had studied throughout her career. She had passed her love of learning and her insatiable curiosity onto Sofia, who always felt both supported and challenged by her mother.

"Good point, Mom," Sofia replied, her eyes scanning the room once more, seeking inspiration from the dusty surroundings. "The symbols don't seem to have any obvious connections to the local culture here in La Porta, but I'll keep that in mind."

"Remember, sometimes it's the most unexpected connections that can lead to the truth," Linette reminded her gently, her voice filled with encouragement.

"Thanks, Mom. I appreciate your input," Sofia said, touched by her mother's unwavering support.

Just as Sofia was about to say her goodbyes, her father chimed in again. "As I say to my archaeology students, context is king. Always, always interpret your discoveries within their proper context. You'll figure it out—I have faith in you."

"Thanks, Dad," Sofia said, grateful to have parents who believed in her and were invested in seeing her succeed.

"Anytime, mija," Emilio replied warmly. "We're always here for you."

"Love you both," Sofia said, her voice thick with gratitude as she ended the call.

As she pocketed her phone, she glanced over at Ryan. He stood with his back to her, his head bent forward as he studied his phone.

"Ryan?" she ventured cautiously, her brows furrowing as she tried to read him. "What's going on?"

He took a deep breath, his broad shoulders rising and falling as he turned to face her. "The coroner just messaged me," he said, his voice tight with concern. "We need to go to the morgue right away. She said there's something...very unusual about the bodies. We're going to want to see this for ourselves."

CHAPTER TWELVE

A sense of unease settled on Sofia as she pulled up to the morgue, Ryan silent in the passenger seat beside her.

What, she wondered, could the coroner have discovered about the bodies to prompt her to urge Sofia and Ryan to come as soon as possible?

The afternoon was getting late, and the fading California sun cast an eerie glow on the building's gray façade.

Sofia felt the hairs on the back of her neck stand up as she opened the car door and stepped onto the pavement. She turned to Ryan, who had been staring out the window, lost in thought.

"Are you coming?" she asked him.

He stirred, shaking his head. "Sorry, just thinking about Hayes's call."

Sofia said nothing as Ryan got out of the car and clapped the door shut. She'd forgotten he'd mentioned updating their boss. Now, however, she wondered how the conversation had gone, especially in light of the chilly reception Hayes had given her when he briefed them about this case.

"How'd that go?" she asked as they approached the building.

Ryan shrugged one shoulder. "Nothing particularly interesting. Just told him how the investigation is going."

Neither said anything for a few moments. Then Sofia asked, "My name didn't come up by any chance, did it?"

Ryan hesitated. "He may have asked me to keep an eye on you."

Sofia shook her head, unable to believe what she was hearing. Why did Hayes always seem to have it out for her? Was it because she was a woman? Was it because she was as sharp as a tack and her intelligence had more than once made him look bad, even though that wasn't her intention?

"Look," Ryan said, raising a placating hand. "As far as I'm concerned, you don't need to be watched, okay? I just agreed so that Hayes would back off. Whatever beef he's got, that's between the two of you."

She found herself smiling wryly, despite her annoyance. "So you're not going to be giving him a play-by-play? Telling him what I'm doing every five minutes?"

Ryan chuckled. "That would be crazy. More like every ten minutes."

Sofia rolled her eyes.

They entered the morgue's sterile lobby, the scent of disinfectant and formaldehyde assaulting Sofia's senses. Her heart pounded in her chest, her stomach twisting with a mix of anticipation and dread as she wondered what evidence the coroner might have discovered.

They headed to a door at the end of the lobby. Sofia pushed it open to reveal a dimly lit chamber lined with steel drawers, each one holding its own macabre secret. A faint hum emanated from the cooling units, filling the room with an unsettling drone. The temperature was noticeably colder here, causing Sofia to shudder, though she wasn't sure if it was from the cold or the atmosphere.

"Agents Blake and Donovan," came a voice from the far side of the room, drawing their attention. Dr. Emily Blackwood emerged from the shadows, her lab coat pristine against the somber backdrop. She was a woman of average height, her dark hair pulled back into a tight bun, revealing sharp, intelligent green eyes that seemed to pierce through them.

"Thank you for coming so quickly," she said, extending a gloved hand in greeting. "I think you need to see this."

The agents followed Dr. Blackwood to a table in the center of the room. Upon it lay the bodies of two young women, their pale skin marred by brutal slashes across their throats. Sofia's heart ached at the gruesome sight, which the harsh fluorescents did nothing to soften. What had these poor women gone through in their final moments?

"Meet our victims," Dr. Blackwood said solemnly as she gestured to the bodies. "The cause of death is self-explanatory. That's not what I wanted to show you, though."

She adjusted her glasses, taking a deep breath before continuing. "I noticed something peculiar about the blood patterns." She pointed to the dried, dark crimson stains on the victims' faces. "See how the blood has pooled around their eyes and noses? This indicates that they were hanging upside down when their throats were cut."

Sofia felt bile rise in her throat at the thought of such cruelty.

"Upside down?" Ryan asked, looking bewildered. "Why would anyone do that?"

Dr. Blackwood shook her head. "I don't know. It's possible that this was some kind of ritualistic killing."

Sofia's mind raced with the possibilities. Was this the work of a cult? A serial killer obeying some twisted ritual?

Then, as Sofia thought about it, she recalled something she had studied once.

"You know," she said softly, "there's an ancient Aztec practice very similar to this."

Both Ryan and Dr. Blackwood studied her.

"Go on," Ryan said. "Don't leave us in suspense."

Sofia cleared her throat. "During my time studying linguistics, I became fascinated with Mesoamerican cultures. The Aztecs believed that offering human sacrifices would appease their gods and ensure the continued survival of their people. One such ritual involved hanging captives upside down, often by their ankles, and having a priest slit their throats with an obsidian knife. The blood would then be collected in ceremonial bowls and used in various rites."

As Sofia spoke, her stomach churned at the thought of the brutal practice. She glanced at Ryan, who wore an equally disturbed expression, before turning back to Dr. Blackwood.

"Of course, I can't say for certain there's a connection," Sofia admitted ruefully. "But given the similarities, it's something worth considering."

"Indeed." Dr. Blackwood nodded solemnly, her eyes darkened with concern.

Nobody said anything for several moments. Then Dr. Blackwood took a quick breath and said, "I noticed something else, as well. Your killer appears to be left-handed."

Sofia's eyebrows furrowed in curiosity. "How can you tell?"

"Notice how the cuts begin at the right side of their necks and angle upward to the left," Dr. Blackwood explained as she gestured with her gloved hand. "The strokes are more hesitant on the right side, while becoming deeper and more confident toward the left. It suggests the use of a left hand, applying more pressure and control as the blade moved across."

"Interesting," Sofia mused, her mind racing with new possibilities. She knew that only a small percentage of the population was left-handed, which could help narrow down their list of suspects.

"Thank you for all your insights, Dr. Blackwood," she said, grateful for the woman's expertise.

"You're welcome, agents," Dr. Blackwood replied, her gaze focused on the two lifeless bodies before her. "I'll let you know if I find anything else of significance."

As they exited the room, the sterile smell of the morgue gave way to the dry, sun-warmed air outside. The late afternoon sun cast long shadows over the parking lot, painting everything in an eerie golden hue. Sofia shivered involuntarily, both from the sudden chill and the lingering dread from what they had just witnessed.

"Maybe we should take a closer look at the contacts of our victims," Ryan suggested, breaking the silence as they made their way to their vehicle. "We might find someone who fits the left-handed profile or has connections to Aztec history or rituals."

"That's not a bad idea," Sofia said.

As she slid behind the wheel of her black Dodge Charger, she couldn't help but wonder: Had the victims been acquainted with their killer? Was this a case of betrayal and murder, or simply the work of a deranged individual obsessed with ancient rituals? And if the killer had targeted individuals he knew, how many others might he know?

And how soon would he pay them a visit?

CHAPTER THIRTEEN

As Sofia steered her black Charger through the narrow lanes of the trailer park, she couldn't help but notice the odd stares directed at them. She felt exposed, like a foreign entity invading a tight-knit community.

The early evening California sun cast long shadows on the rows of weather-beaten trailers, some adorned with fading murals and others with peeling paint. The scent of marigolds and candles filled the air, mingling with the aroma of cooking food from various outdoor grills. Children darted between trailers, their faces painted as calaveras, laughing, and playing with sugar skulls.

Sofia wondered what it was like for the Limas to grieve the loss of Roberta, surrounded by all these symbols of death.

"Ryan, remind me which trailer we're looking for?" Sofia asked, her eyes scanning the area.

"Uh, hang on," he replied, pulling out his phone and swiping at the screen. "Two-hundred-thirty-seven Hawthorne Lane."

Sofia frowned, squinting at the numbers on the trailers as they drove by. Nothing seemed to match the address she was looking for. It was as if the Lima family's home was deliberately hidden from view.

"Are you sure that's the right address?" she asked, her grip tightening on the steering wheel. "I can't seem to find it."

"Positive," Ryan said, double-checking the information on his phone. "Maybe one of the locals can point us in the right direction."

Sofia's gaze fell upon a group of people gathered around a fire, their faces illuminated by the flickering flames. The motley crew consisted of men and women of varying ages, some with intricately painted faces in homage to Día de los Muertos. A couple of elderly women sat on folding chairs, murmuring among themselves, while a younger man strummed a guitar, his fingers dancing nimbly over the strings. The atmosphere was one of camaraderie and shared memories, and Sofia felt as if she were intruding on something sacred.

Taking a deep breath, she stepped out of her Charger and approached the group cautiously. The murmurs died down, the guitar music coming to an abrupt halt as all eyes turned toward her. It was as if the fire had been doused, leaving only a heavy silence in its wake.

"Excuse me," Sofia began, trying her best to sound friendly despite the tension that hung in the air like a dense fog. "We're looking for the Lima family. Can any of you help us find them?"

A heavyset woman with graying hair pulled back into a tight bun spoke up, her dark eyes narrowing suspiciously. Her cheeks were adorned with colorful flower designs, and her ample frame was clad in a vibrant red dress that accentuated her presence.

"Who are you?" she demanded, her voice thick with a Hispanic accent. "What do you want with the Limas?"

Sofia held her hands up in a placating gesture. "My name is Sofia Blake, and this is my partner Ryan Donovan. We're with the FBI. We're investigating Roberta Lima's murder, and we need to speak with her family."

"Roberta?" the woman repeated, her voice wavering ever so slightly. "The police have already harassed them enough. They need time to grieve in peace."

Sofia could see the genuine concern in the woman's eyes, and she knew that the woman was only trying to protect the Limas from further heartache. She wished she could promise that their visit wouldn't bring any more pain, but truthfully, she couldn't guarantee anything.

"Please," she implored, her voice softening. "We just want to help Roberta's family find closure. If you could point us in the right direction, we'd be very grateful."

The heavyset woman held her gaze for a long moment, as if weighing the sincerity of Sofia's words against the potential harm they might cause. The silence around the fire seemed to stretch on indefinitely, broken only by the distant laughter of children and the crackle of burning logs.

Ryan, sensing the woman's hesitation, stepped in. "I understand your concern," he said, his voice steady and reassuring. "But the Limas will never truly have closure until the person who murdered Roberta is caught. We just want to find justice for her."

Still the woman hesitated. She seemed to be trying to come up with reasons why she shouldn't direct them to the Limas, as if she sincerely believed the only good they could do was to leave the grieving family alone.

Just then, while Sofia was contemplating how else to try to convince the woman, a young man by the fire spoke up. He had been silent until now, his eyes downcast as he poked at the embers with a stick. "The Limas live over there," he said, pointing down the street. "It's the green trailer with the faded numbers on it."

"Javier!" the heavyset woman snapped, glaring at him. "What are you trying to do, make them relive Roberta's death all over again?"

"Someone needs to find the person who killed her," Javier said with a defensive shrug. "Don't you think we should at least try to help?"

"Thank you, Javier," Ryan said, ignoring the woman's scolding tone. He exchanged a glance with Sofia, who offered the young man a warm smile.

As they walked away from the group, Sofia felt a sudden chill in the air, making her shiver involuntarily. The sun was setting, casting long shadows across the ground, and the faces of the people they left behind seemed to blur together like watercolor paintings.

As they neared the trailer, Sofia turned to Ryan. "I think that woman really believed she was protecting the Limas," she said thoughtfully.

"You're probably right," Ryan agreed, his voice soft and understanding. "If it was her daughter that was murdered, though, I suspect she'd care a little more about justice and a little less about peace and quiet."

Sofia nodded, her heart aching for the family they were about to visit. She knew their lives had been shattered by Roberta's murder, and she hoped their presence would ultimately serve as a balm, rather than an irritant.

The green trailer came into view as they rounded a bend, its faded numbers barely visible on the door. It was evident from the peeling paint and overgrown yard that the residents hadn't been tending to it with much care. The tires of a tricycle lay half-buried in the weeds, while colorful chalk drawings adorned the patchy sidewalk nearby.

"I'm guessing Roberta had some younger siblings," Ryan said, his eyes lingering on the abandoned toys scattered across the yard.

"I can't imagine what they're going through," Sofia murmured, her gaze following a trail of ants crawling along the edge of a hopscotch grid. She wondered how many times Roberta must have played with her younger siblings here before her life was snuffed out so abruptly.

Gathering her resolve, Sofia rapped sharply on the trailer door. The sound was loud in the still evening air, mingling with the distant laughter of children playing a few trailers down. For a moment, there was only silence, as though the world itself was holding its breath.

Then, with a barely perceptible creak, the door opened, revealing a man who appeared to be in his mid-forties. His face was etched with lines that spoke of many sleepless nights, and his eyes were rimmed with red, as though he had been crying. He stepped out onto the stoop, closing the door gently behind him, and glanced quickly at Sofia and Ryan before fixing his gaze on the ground.

"Sorry," he murmured, his voice hushed. "I just put the kids down for the night. Are you detectives?"

Sofia exchanged a glance with Ryan before answering. "Actually, we're with the FBI," she said softly, extending a hand. "I'm Special Agent Sofia Blake, and this is my partner, Special Agent Ryan Donovan."

The man looked at her outstretched hand for a moment, then shook it slowly, almost hesitantly. "Michael Lima," he replied, managing a faint smile. "Roberta's father."

"Mr. Lima, do you mind if we ask you a few questions about your daughter?"

He nodded, his eyes grave. "Of course. Anything to help you find the person responsible for taking her away from us."

Sofia studied Michael's weary features before diving into her questions. "Was Roberta dating anyone at the time of her death?" she asked.

Michael shook his head slowly. "No, not that I know of. She had a few friends, but no serious relationships, not recently."

"Can you describe her mood in the days leading up to her death? Did you notice any changes in her behavior?"

He sighed, rubbing a hand over his face. "She seemed...distant. Maybe a little stressed. But nothing too out of the ordinary. We all have our ups and downs, right?"

"Of course," Sofia agreed, nodding sympathetically. "Did she mention having problems with anyone? Anyone who might have had a reason to hurt her?"

"Everyone loved Roberta," Michael said, his voice cracking with emotion. "She had a kind heart—always trying to help others. I've got a four-year-old and a six-year-old, and they both loved Roberta to death. We all did."

"Is her mother still in the picture?" Ryan asked.

Michael shook his head. "We divorced a few years ago, shortly after my youngest was born. She was..." He pursed his lips. "A bad influence on the kids. When I came home from work one day and found her passed out on the couch, high as a kite while the kids screamed for her attention—well, that was when I knew things had to change. The divorce was difficult on Roberta, but—"

A child's cry pierced the air from inside the trailer. Michael's attention snapped toward the door, his expression laced with concern. "I'm sorry, I have to go."

"Of course," Sofia said, stepping back to allow him space. But as he reached for the doorknob, a thought struck her. "One quick question, Mr. Lima. You mentioned that Roberta hadn't had any serious relationships recently. When was the last time she dated?"

Michael paused, one hand on the door, the other clenched into a fist. He seemed to be weighing his options as the sound of the child's cries grew louder. Finally, he sighed and turned to face Sofia once more. "There was this guy, Todd Snyder. They dated for about six months, broke up a week or so ago. He sent her some threatening letters, even stopped by a time or two and demanded to speak with her. I told him to go pound sand, of course."

"Do you know where we can find him?"

"Try Haslem Brothers—it's an automotive shop downtown. Now I really have to get going."

"Thank you, Mr. Lima," Sofia replied, her mind already racing with possibilities. "We'll look into it. And again, we're so sorry for your loss."

As Michael slipped back inside the trailer, leaving the agents standing in the dim twilight, Sofia couldn't shake the feeling that there was more to this story than met the eye.

It was time to track down this Todd Snyder and find out what it was.

CHAPTER FOURTEEN

Sofia leaned against the hood of her car as she focused on the mechanics working inside Haslem Brothers Automotive.

Where are you, Todd Snyder? she thought.

The fading sunlight splashed a golden hue across the garage floor, casting long shadows from the vehicles. From her vantage point, Sofia could see oil-stained concrete and various tools scattered haphazardly around the workstations. The smell of grease and gasoline permeated the air, while the distant hum of traffic outside served as a constant reminder that they were still in the heart of the city.

"Any sign of him?" Ryan asked, his blue eyes scanning the photo of Todd Snyder he held in his hand.

"Nothing yet," she replied, observing the mechanics who worked sluggishly, their movements betraying their eagerness to call it a day and head home. One man with tattooed arms wiped the sweat off his brow with the back of his hand, leaving a faint smudge of grease. Another mechanic, a woman with short-cropped hair, rolled out from under a car, her face streaked with oil and fatigue.

"Let's ask around," Ryan suggested, pushing himself off from the side of the car.

As they approached the entrance, Sofia noticed a mechanic smoking just outside. He was a middle-aged man with salt-and-pepper hair and a five o'clock shadow that seemed to have started at noon. His eyes were tired and bloodshot, and his uniform was wrinkled, as if it hadn't seen an iron in years.

"Excuse me," Sofia said, flashing her FBI badge. "We're looking for Todd Snyder. Do you know if he's here?"

The mechanic took a long drag of his cigarette before exhaling a cloud of smoke. "Todd?" he scoffed. "He better not be around here."

"Mind if I ask why?" Sofia asked, her curiosity piqued.

"Because he was fired a few days ago," the man explained, his voice gruff and annoyed. "He messed up a transmission job on a customer's car. Cost us a fortune to fix it—and even more in lost business."

As they talked, the sounds of the shop continued in the background. The hiss of a compressor filled the air, accompanied by the rhythmic clank of wrenches turning bolts. A stereo blared classic rock somewhere inside, adding to the cacophony of noise that surrounded them.

"Any idea where we might find him?" Sofia asked.

"Couldn't tell you," the mechanic replied, taking one last drag before flicking his cigarette onto the pavement.

"Is there anyone else here who might know where Todd is?" Ryan asked.

The man scratched his stubbly chin, thinking for a moment before pointing toward the back of the shop. "Cynthia might know. She's over there, working on that blue sedan."

"Thank you," Sofia replied, nodding her appreciation as she and Ryan headed in the direction he had indicated.

As they approached Cynthia, Sofia watched the woman carefully maneuver a hydraulic jack beneath the car, her face set in concentration. Her dark hair was pulled back into a tight ponytail, and a smudge of grease streaked across her forehead. The sleeves of her coveralls were rolled up, revealing toned arms that spoke of years spent working with heavy machinery.

"Hi, there," Sofia began, flashing her FBI badge as she had earlier. "We're looking for Todd Snyder, and we heard you might be able to help us find him."

Cynthia glanced up from her task, her eyes narrowing in annoyance. It was clear she wasn't thrilled about being interrupted just as her shift was nearing its end. "What do you want with Todd?" she asked warily, wiping her hands on a dirty rag.

"We're investigating a case he may be involved in," Ryan explained. "Any information you can give us would be greatly appreciated."

Cynthia sighed heavily, her shoulders slumping as she realized she wasn't going to get out of this conversation easily. "Fine," she muttered. "But I don't have all day, so let's make this quick."

"Of course," Sofia assured her, trying to ease some of the tension. "How well do you know Todd Snyder?"

Cynthia snorted, a bitter twist to her lips. "Too well, believe me. Haven't seen him since he quit, though. Good riddance."

Sofia caught the edge of resentment in Cynthia's voice and decided to probe further. "You sound upset. Did something happen between you two?"

Cynthia hesitated for a moment before sighing, her shoulders sagging under the weight of her confession. "Todd and I...we dated for a little while. But he treated me like crap. Belittled me constantly, tried to control what I wore, who I talked to. Even here at work, he'd undermine me in front of the other mechanics." Bitterness seeped into her every word.

"Do you have any idea where we can find him now?" Ryan asked.

"Sometimes he goes to this bar called the Rusty Wrench," Cynthia said, her gaze flicking away from theirs. "It's not too far from here."

"Can you describe him for us?" Sofia asked gently, wanting to make sure they had the right person in mind when searching the bar.

"Dark hair, usually slicked back, a thin mustache. He has this smug, self-satisfied expression most of the time. If just looking at him makes you want to slap him, it's probably Todd."

"Thank you, Cynthia," Sofia said, offering a small smile. "We'll let you get back to work." She turned to leave. She had only gone a few paces, however, before Cynthia's voice stopped her.

"Hey," Cynthia called, her voice hesitant. "Just...be careful if you're going to talk with Todd, okay?"

Ryan frowned. "Why's that?"

"He can get nasty when he drinks. Violent." She shook her head bitterly. "Believe me, I would know."

* * *

"Dark hair slicked back, thin mustache," Sofia murmured to Ryan as they scanned the crowd, searching for any sign of Todd Snyder among the sea of faces.

"Got it," Ryan replied, his eyes narrowing slightly as he focused on their task, the muscles in his broad shoulders tensing beneath his jacket.

The interior of the bar was a study in contrasts. Weathered wooden beams stretched across the ceiling, juxtaposed against the sleek chrome of the bar counter and the polished glass bottles that gleamed in the low light. A worn jukebox stood sentinel in one corner, its tinny music providing a soundtrack to the muffled conversations that filled the air.

The low hum of conversation swelled around Sofia as she and Ryan threaded their way through the throng of patrons. The dim lighting cast a moody, almost ominous atmosphere over the bar, with shadows flickering in the corners as the early evening crowd jostled for position at the counter or sought refuge in the dingy booths lining the walls.

"Let's split up," Sofia said to Ryan, her dark eyes darting from one face to another, searching for any sign of the man Cynthia had described. "I'll take this side, you go that way. We'll cover more ground."

"Be careful," Ryan said, his voice barely audible above the din of clinking glasses and laughter. They exchanged a brief nod and then went their separate ways.

Sofia wove her way between clusters of people, her senses heightened, acutely aware of every hushed conversation and sidelong glance that seemed to follow her path. It was as though the very air of the bar held secrets, whispers of unsavory deeds and hidden threats lurking just beneath the surface.

And then she saw him—a solitary figure seated in a shadowy corner, his features partially obscured by the glass he cradled in one hand. He matched Cynthia's description: dark hair, a thin mustache, and an air of smug arrogance even in his slumped posture. This had to be Todd.

"Todd Snyder?" Sofia asked, her voice steady despite the rapid beat of her pulse. The man looked up, his eyes wide with surprise—and perhaps a flicker of fear.

"Who's asking?" he replied, his voice guarded.

"Special Agent Sofia Blake, FBI," she said, flashing her badge. "I have a few questions for you."

Todd's eyes darted around the room as if searching for an escape route or a hidden ally, but he remained seated. "What do you want to know?"

"Roberta Lima," Sofia began, watching his face closely for any sign of recognition or guilt. "How did you know her?"

"Roberta?" Todd's voice wavered slightly, betraying his nerves. "We...we dated for a while."

"Why did you break up?" Sofia pressed, leaning in closer, her gaze never leaving his face.

"Mutual decision," he mumbled, avoiding her eyes. "We just...decided it was best to part ways. Friendly terms, nothing more." His words felt rehearsed, as if he'd prepared himself for this very question. But something in his demeanor told Sofia there was more to the story than what Todd was willing to divulge.

"Michael Lima, Roberta's father, had a different take on your relationship," Sofia said. "He claimed you sent her harassing letters."

Todd's face flushed with anger, his eyes narrowing as he clenched his fists. "That's a lie! I never did anything like that!"

Sofia could feel the tension in the air, thick and charged like static electricity before a storm. She knew she needed to tread carefully, lest this situation spiral out of control. "Todd, I'm not accusing you of anything," she explained calmly, trying to diffuse his rising temper. "I'm simply trying to gather all the information I can to piece together what happened to Roberta."

But Todd was already too agitated to listen, his breathing heavy and his knuckles white from gripping the edges of the table. "I'm done talking!" he snapped, pushing himself to his feet. His chair scraped loudly against the floor, drawing the attention of nearby patrons.

Before Todd could make his way through the crowd, however, Ryan appeared, seemingly out of nowhere, blocking his path. He stood tall and imposing, his arms crossed over his broad chest. He clucked his tongue in a chiding way. "It's not very polite, talking to a lady that way."

Todd's face contorted with frustration, his jaw clenching and unclenching as he fought to keep his anger in check. But Sofia could see the fear lurking beneath the surface, the uncertainty of what might happen if he didn't cooperate.

"What do you want from me?" he growled, his eyes darting between Sofia and Ryan, the muscles in his neck tense with irritation.

Sofia leveled her gaze at him. "We're investigating Roberta Lima's death. She was murdered two days ago."

At the mention of Roberta's fate, Todd's face drained of color and he seemed to deflate, the anger seeping out of him like air from a punctured balloon. "I...I didn't know she was dead," he stammered, sounding shocked.

"Where were you two days ago?" Sofia asked, studying him closely for any hint of deception.

"Two days ago?" Todd echoed, the gears visibly turning in his head as he tried to recall his whereabouts. "I was working at another garage. They called me in to help with an engine overhaul that was taking longer than expected." He swallowed hard, his voice cracking slightly. "You can check with them if you don't believe me. The owner's name is Carlos."

Sofia noted the alibi, mentally filing it away for later verification. If true, it would clear Todd of any involvement in Roberta's murder.

As Ryan continued to question Todd about his relationship with Roberta and any potential enemies she might have had, Sofia's phone vibrated in her pocket, signaling an incoming call. She excused herself from the conversation, stepping away to answer. "Agent Blake speaking."

"Agent Blake, this is Detective Alvarez from the local precinct," the voice on the other end of the line informed her, a sense of urgency lacing his tone. "We've got another murder on our hands, and I think it's connected to the Calavera Killer."

Sofia's heart clenched at the news. *So they've already got a celebrity name for the killer,* she thought grimly.

"Are you absolutely certain it's connected?" she asked.

"Oh, there's little doubt," Alvarez replied. "Last I checked, it wasn't common practice to leave a calavera on the body of someone you just murdered."

CHAPTER FIFTEEN

Sofia scanned the painted faces and elaborate costumes of the La Porta revelers, a shiver running down her spine.

Is the killer here, hiding in plain sight? she wondered. *He wouldn't even need a mask, since we don't know what he looks like.*

"Quite a scene, isn't it?" Ryan said, as if reading her thoughts.

Sofia nodded, unable to shake off the unsettling feeling that had taken hold of her. "It's strange that a celebration can be so beautiful and terrifying at the same time. Every time I meet someone's eyes, I find myself wondering if it might be the last pair of eyes the victims saw."

Ryan rubbed his chin, looking thoughtful. "It's only a matter of time before we find him. He'll mess up eventually—they always do."

Sofia said nothing. Inwardly she was wondering how many more lives the killer would take before making that crucial mistake.

As they got out of the car, Sofia heard someone call her name. She turned to see Ethan Knight waving to them, his face solemn in the fading light.

"Agent Blake, Agent Donovan," he said in a subdued voice by way of greeting. "It's good to see you again, though I wish it were under different circumstances."

"Me too," Sofia replied, steeling herself for what lay ahead. She knew that beneath Ethan's calm exterior, he was just as shaken by the grisly murders that had brought them here as she was.

"Come on, I'll lead you to the body," Ethan said. He turned and began to walk away. Sofia followed closely behind, her heart heavy with dread.

As Sofia and Ryan followed Ethan through the narrow cobblestone alleys of La Porta, the vibrant colors of the Día de los Muertos decorations seemed to lose their cheerfulness. The music and laughter of the festivities grew fainter until they were replaced by the harsh sound of police radios crackling in the air.

As they turned a corner, Sofia saw the secluded place where the third victim had been found—a small courtyard tucked between two crumbling buildings. Yellow crime scene tape cordoned off the area, its stark contrast to the festive surroundings a chilling reminder of the horror that had unfolded here. Police officers in uniform milled about, conversing in hushed voices. A forensic photographer knelt beside the body, capturing every detail of the gruesome scene, while curious spectators huddled just outside the tape, whispering among themselves.

The young woman lay in a pool of her own blood on the cold ground, her throat slashed open by an unforgiving blade. Her face was pale, her dark hair framing her lifeless eyes like a macabre halo. A calavera sat atop her chest, a sinister mockery of the sugar skulls that adorned the town's altars and offerings.

Sofia's stomach twisted into knots at the sight. She swallowed hard, forcing herself to focus on the task at hand. Crouching down, she examined the calavera with a practiced eye.

"This is exactly like the other one we found," she said. She traced her fingers over the intricate designs on the skull, feeling the carved grooves beneath her fingertips. "There's no doubt in my mind that this is the work of the same killer."

"Three victims now," Ryan murmured, his blue eyes clouded with concern. "He's escalating, Sofia. We need to notify town officials, send out a warning that there's a killer stalking the streets. We don't exactly have jurisdiction to just shut the town down – and that would probably scare the killer off, anyway – but we need to do *something*."

Sofia couldn't help but agree. As she studied the calavera and the lifeless body before her, a sense of urgency settled heavily on her shoulders. The killer was growing bolder, more violent, and time was running out for them to stop him.

Ethan's voice cut through the eerie silence. "Her name was Martina Alvarez," he said, his voice tight with emotion. "She worked at the local library and was last seen leaving work just a few hours ago."

Ryan furrowed his brow, studying the young woman's lifeless form. "Who found her?" he asked, his voice betraying the anger simmering beneath the surface.

"A group of children playing nearby stumbled upon her. A terrible shame, innocent kids being exposed to a sight like this."

Sofia's heart ached for the innocent lives touched by this brutal act. She knew they needed to act quickly if they were to prevent more bloodshed. "We have three victims now, all discovered within as many days," she said. "It seems pretty clear that our killer isn't going to stop until we make him."

"Any ideas on how we might track him down?" Ryan asked.

Ethan ran a hand through his dark hair, his forehead creased in thought. "Well, the calavera seems to be a significant symbol for the killer. Maybe there's something about it that can give us a clue to his identity or whereabouts."

"Or perhaps there's a pattern to his killings, a connection between the victims that might lead us to him," Sofia mused, her mind racing as she considered every possibility.

"Whatever it is, we need to figure it out soon," Ryan added, his gaze sweeping over the scene once more. "The clock is ticking, and we can't afford to let this murderer claim any more lives."

As the sun dipped lower in the sky and shadows lengthened around them, Sofia felt a chill run down her spine at the thought of the relentless predator stalking the streets of La Porta. They needed to uncover his secrets, decipher the twisted message woven into the calaveras, and bring him to justice.

And they needed to do it quickly before more innocent lives were snuffed out like candles in the encroaching darkness.

She crouched beside the body, her father's voice from their earlier conversation echoing in her mind: *As I say to my archaeology students, context is king. Always, always interpret your discoveries within their proper context.*

So what was the context of these calaveras?

Think, Sofia, think! she told herself.

She suspected that the key to stopping the killer was hidden somewhere within the details of the murders. Her mind raced as she considered every clue they had gathered so far. The calaveras were clearly significant to the killer, but why? Was it a personal fascination with Día de los Muertos, or was there a deeper meaning to the symbols? She traced her fingers over the intricate designs of the skull again, her mind searching for patterns.

"He's a visionary," she murmured.

"What was that?" Ryan asked.

Sofia looked up. "The killer. He's a visionary. I don't think he's using these skulls because he thinks they're cool or because it's just the right time of year. He clearly timed these murders to this festival, to these two days."

Ryan frowned. "He didn't leave a calavera on the first one," he said. "And besides, he killed her before the festival even started."

Always, Sofia heard her father say, *always interpret your discoveries within their proper context.*

She snapped her fingers as a revelation came to her. "He was practicing," she said, glancing from Ryan to Ethan, her eyes bright. "He was—"

"Doing a dry run," Ethan finished for her, nodding. "Figuring out how he wanted to do it."

Sofia nodded back at him. "The skulls—they're important, part of whatever ritual he's enacting. I think he takes the Day of the Dead very seriously, maybe even to the point that he thinks he's honoring his ancestors somehow."

"Honoring his ancestors?" Ryan asked skeptically. "You think that's what this is all about?"

She shrugged. "I don't know. But whatever it is...I think he's following some type of vision, some type of path that's been laid out for him. And if I had to guess, I'd say the secret to understanding the path he's on lies with the skulls."

Ethan was nodding slowly, his eyes bright with interest. "What do you say we compare the two skulls, see if we can't piece together his message?"

CHAPTER SIXTEEN

Santo's hands closed around the woman's wrists, forcing them together behind her back. He twisted the rough rope around her delicate skin, feeling a surge of triumph as he tightened the knot.

She squirmed beneath him, her breaths coming in short, sharp gasps as she tried to wriggle free. But Santo held her firmly in place, his knee digging into her spine and pinning her down like a butterfly to a display board.

"Stop struggling," he growled, a sinister smile playing at the corners of his mouth. "You're only making this harder on yourself."

The basement of the butcher's shop was dimly lit, the air thick with the scent of blood and raw meat. Hooks dangled from the ceiling, their metal surfaces slick and gleaming in the dull light. The floor beneath them was cold and unforgiving, stained with dark patches that bore testament to the grisly work performed within these walls.

Outside, the night was alive with the sounds of Día de los Muertos. The rhythmic beat of drums mingled with laughter and singing, punctuated by the occasional burst of fireworks. The narrow window set high along the wall offered Santo a glimpse of the celebrations unfolding just beyond his reach. Colorful skirts swirled past, accompanied by the tapping of heels and the rustle of silk. Human legs danced and moved in the shadows, oblivious to the darkness that lurked just beneath them.

"Pathetic, isn't it?" Santo mused, his eyes fixed on the small square of life visible through the glass. "All those people out there, celebrating death without any idea of what it really means."

They had even been warned about him. Santo had heard the warning himself from a vendor: apparently there was a "dangerous killer" out "stalking the streets." And yet, nobody seemed to care. It was as if nobody thought they could be the next person he targeted.

Santo turned his attention back to the woman beneath him, watching as she fought to keep her composure. There would be time enough to break her spirit later; for now, he had other plans.

He was expecting her to break into tears or plead for mercy. But to his surprise, she did nothing of the sort. Her chest heaved with each breath, but her eyes burned with defiance. She was a fighter, and it sent a shiver of excitement down his spine.

Breaking strong spirits was always more satisfying.

"Tell me," the woman said, her voice strained but steady. "What do you plan to do with me?"

Santo couldn't help but grin at her audacity. He leaned in close, his breath hot against her cheek. "You'll learn soon enough, my dear."

She turned her head away from him, disgust etched across her features. "Pathetic," she said. "You amuse yourself with others' pain because you don't know how to love or be loved. You would rather hurt than risk being hurt. I despise people like you."

His face darkened, anger flaring within him. How dare she speak to him this way? Did she not know who he was? What he was capable of?

"Your disdain means nothing to me," Santo growled. "Soon, you'll be begging for mercy. And you will find none here."

The woman met his gaze, unflinching even in the face of his fury. It was an act of courage that both infuriated and intrigued him. He could tell there was something different about her, something he hadn't encountered in his previous victims. This one would not break so easily, and he relished the challenge.

"Go ahead, then. Do your worst," she said, her tone laced with contempt. "But remember: every action has consequences. Even for monsters like you."

Santo's rage bubbled as he listened to the woman's biting words. Clenching his jaw, he grabbed hold of a hook hanging from the ceiling, attached to a pulley system designed for hoisting slabs of meat. As he fastened the hook to her ankle bindings, Santo imagined her swinging upside down like a side of beef, helpless and humiliated.

"Let's see how brave you are now," he sneered, preparing to lift her off the ground. But just as he was about to set the pulley in motion, a pounding sound boomed through the basement, originating from the door leading out to the street. His heart skipped a beat, and his eyes darted toward the source of the noise.

"Stay quiet," he hissed at the woman, covering her mouth with a bandanna before swiftly ascending the stairs to investigate the disturbance.

As he reached the top of the stairs and opened the door, Santo was met by a trio of women standing on the street outside. They were middle-aged and smiling, their faces partly covered by artistic masks.

"Is the butcher shop open?" inquired the first, a short woman with a pixie haircut, her voice tinged with curiosity. "I know it's late, but we were hoping to—"

"Closed," Santo said quickly. "You'll have to come back tomorrow."

The women exchanged glances, disappointment etched on their faces. The second woman, tall and raven-haired, stepped forward, crossing her arms, and furrowing her brow. "Are you sure? We really need something for our celebration tonight."

"Positive," Santo said, his patience hanging on by a thread. "I'm just cleaning up. I'm an assistant, you see—not the owner."

The third woman, of middling height and wearing a sombrero with tassels, cleared her throat. "You couldn't make an exception, just this once?"

Santo sighed, trying his best to look regretful. "Afraid not. I'd lose my job if my boss found out. He's a very strict man, you see. Always goes by the book."

The woman with the sombrero nodded, looking resigned. "Alright," she said as she began to turn. "Well, it looks like we'll just have to—"

A muffled scream pierced through the air, rising from the depths of the basement. The three women froze. Santo felt a jolt of panic, beads of sweat forming on his brow as he scrambled for an excuse.

"Ah, that's nothing," he said, forcing a smile to his lips. "Just a pig. I was in the middle of slaughtering it when you knocked, you see. It's just dangling down there, awaiting its fate." He chuckled.

But the women were not easily deterred. The raven-haired one narrowed her eyes, suspicion clouding her features. "I thought you said you were cleaning up," she replied, her voice laced with doubt.

Santo's heart hammered against his chest. His grip tightened on the door handle, knuckles turning white as he fought to maintain control.

"Cleaning up?" he repeated. "No, I meant to say *finishing* up. I'll just butcher this one, and then I'm done for the night." *Which isn't too far from the truth,* he added mentally.

The three women exchanged nervous glances, clearly not convinced by Santo's explanation. Did they realize he was the very person they'd been warned about?

Then the sound came again: a muffled scream. The raven-haired woman stepped forward, determination etched across her face. "I'm going down there."

The two others nodded. Santo felt his world crumble around him as the women headed toward him, ready to shove him aside and storm the basement.

"You don't want to do that," he said quickly.

The raven-haired woman stopped and regarded him doubtfully. "Oh, yeah? Why's that?"

He smiled. "You've never seen a pig slaughtered before, have you? They don't go easy, oh no—they thrash and scream, wild as the day they were born. Almost sound human, too. This one's not cut yet, but he knows what's coming, believe me, and he'll shriek to high hell—until he bleeds out, that is."

The woman hesitated, studying him closely as if unsure whether to believe him or not.

He shrugged, as if it didn't matter to him one way or the other. "But, if you don't mind the blood, the stench of offal, and a squirming, grunting pig hanging upside down by its feet..." He sighed theatrically and stepped aside, gesturing for them to go down. "Be my guest."

The woman hesitated a few moments longer. She seemed to be listening, perhaps waiting to see whether the scream would be repeated. To Santo's relief, it didn't come again.

Finally the woman shook herself and gave Santo a thin smile. "Tomorrow, then," she said, and with that, she and her two friends moved along.

Santo exhaled in relief as the women disappeared into the darkening street. He shut the door, sliding the deadbolt into place with a sigh. He heard the muffled sound of footsteps from the basement, and the woman began shouting through the gag in an attempt to attract attention.

"Shut up!" Santo snapped at the woman, barely able to contain his rage. He stomped down the stairs, his face alight with rage. "Do you have any idea how close those women were to discovering our little secret here—and what would have happened if they had?"

The woman's eyes narrowed, clearly understanding his words, even through the haze of fear and pain that enveloped her. She refused to cower before him, her fierce gaze never leaving his face. The spirit within her was admirable, but it would be her undoing.

"Ah, well," Santo said, a twisted grin playing on his lips. "Let's get on with it, shall we?"

He approached her, the hook glinting ominously in the dim light of the basement. As he secured it around her ankles, he couldn't help but admire her resilience. What a waste, he thought, as he prepared to hoist her up like a piece of meat ready for butchering.

"Consider yourself fortunate," Santo murmured, his breath hot against her ear as he began to lift her upside down. "You've been chosen to participate in something far greater than yourself. It's quite an honor."

The pulley system groaned under the weight of her body, which now hung suspended above the cold cement floor. Every muscle seemed to tense in her form as she tried to make sense of her gruesome fate. Santo watched her intently, savoring the terror that began to seep into her eyes.

"Fight it all you want," he whispered, almost tenderly. "But soon, you'll understand. You'll see the importance, the necessity of all this."

As he stepped back to admire his handiwork, the woman's world now turned upside down, Santo felt a perverse satisfaction. He had regained control of the situation, putting her in her place. All that remained was to finish what he had started.

And no one would stand in his way.

CHAPTER SEVENTEEN

Sofia's eyes narrowed as she studied the two calaveras, her fingers hovering just above their smooth surfaces.

"As far as I can tell," she murmured, "they're identical. No difference whatsoever."

The evidence room was a study in organized chaos, with shelves of carefully labeled boxes and bags stretching to the high ceiling. The air was heavy with the scent of dust and stale coffee, punctuated by the occasional whiff of something more sinister—the lingering ghosts of past crimes, perhaps. A long table with a stainless steel top stood in the middle of the room, its cold surface gleaming beneath the harsh fluorescent lights, and it was here that the two calaveras from the crime scenes sat side by side, their hollow eyes seeming to stare straight through Sofia.

Ryan, her FBI partner, stood at one end of the table, his tall frame hunched over as he examined the skulls in tandem with Sofia. A hint of stubble shadowed his strong jawline, giving him the appearance of a man who'd been working nonstop for days, even though the case had begun just that morning.

Ethan Knight, the expert in Mesoamerican languages they had brought in to assist with the case, paced restlessly on the other side of the room. His intelligent eyes seemed to search every corner of the evidence room for the answers that eluded them all.

"That's what I thought, too," Ethan said, approaching the table again. "I was hoping that maybe we could combine the two skulls together and the symbols would start to make sense, but that doesn't seem to be the case."

Ryan looked from Sofia to Ethan, then back again. "Wait a minute," he said. "You're surprised that the skulls left by a sociopath on his victims don't make sense? Does any part of what he's doing make sense?"

"He's a sociopath, yes," Sofia said, rubbing her forehead wearily, "but that doesn't make him a fool. He knows how to think logically, even if that logic has nothing to do with the morals most of us operate within."

"It has to be a message," Ethan muttered, his eyes boring into the skulls. Suddenly he stood up straighter, his eyes brightening. "We could try bringing in experts on Mesoamerican symbolism. They might see something we've missed."

"Or we could talk to some locals," Ryan suggested. "See if there's any cultural significance or folklore tied to these skulls."

"Maybe we should also look into where the skulls themselves came from," Ethan added. "Figure out whether the killer made them or bought them."

As they brainstormed, Sofia couldn't help but feel a creeping sense of frustration. None of the ideas seemed particularly promising, and each one only led to more questions. She clenched her fists, nails biting into her palms, as she tried to suppress her growing agitation.

"Whatever direction we take," she said, "we need to act quickly. We only have one more day of the festival, and it's possible that if he finished whatever ritual he's enacting, he'll disappear forever."

Her fingers drummed on the cold steel table, her brow furrowed in thought. The room seemed to close in around them, as if the sterile walls and dim lighting were a manifestation of the ever-growing pressure to solve this enigmatic case. The scent of disinfectant hung heavy in the air, causing her to wrinkle her nose.

"I just don't get it," Ethan said, shaking his head as he stared at the skulls. "It looks so close to writing...but it's like part of it is missing. I just can't figure out whether that's deliberate or somehow a mistake."

"Wait a minute," Ryan said suddenly, his eyes narrowing. "What if the killer used invisible ink? Something that would only show up under a black light?"

Ethan's skepticism was evident in the arch of his brow. "Invisible ink? That seems a bit...contrived, don't you think?"

"Maybe," Sofia said slowly, considering the possibility. "But it's worth a shot. We have nothing else to go on right now. Where can we get a black light?"

"Someone here must have one," Ryan replied. "I'll go look." With that, he strode purposefully from the evidence room, leaving Sofia and Ethan alone.

As the door clicked shut behind Ryan, an unexpected silence fell between Sofia and Ethan. She could sense his presence beside her even without looking. Their shared passion for linguistics had created an undeniable connection, and she couldn't help but feel a spark of attraction.

Ethan took a deep breath and let it out slowly. "Can't say this was how I expected my week to go."

Sofia smiled. "Do you consult on a lot of cases?"

"Not a lot," Ethan replied, his gaze fixed on the skulls. "And certainly nothing quite like this investigation. I must say, this whole thing kind of makes me feel like a kid again." He hesitated, as if sensing he'd made a faux pas. "That sounds terrible, being invigorated by something so horrible."

"No, I get it. It's both at the same time—horrifying and invigorating."

"That's right," he said, a look of appreciation entering his eyes as he studied her.

Sofia's heartbeat kicked up a notch. She sensed the tension building between them, a palpable electricity that seemed to thrum in the air. As the silence stretched on, she found herself struggling to come up with something to say—anything to break the spell.

Suddenly, the door burst open and Ryan strode back into the room, a small black light in his hand. "Got it," he said, holding it up triumphantly. "Let's see if this works."

"Great," Sofia said, her voice cracking slightly as she struggled to regain her composure. She cleared her throat and straightened her posture, focusing her mind on the task at hand.

"Let's see if he left any secret messages for us to find," Ryan said as he flicked on the black light. A purplish glow filled the room, casting shadows that danced ominously along the walls.

Sofia leaned in closer to the calaveras, her heart pounding with anticipation as she searched for any sign of hidden symbols. Her breath caught in her throat as faint, intricate markings began to materialize under the black light's beam.

"Look at this," she whispered, unable to mask the excitement in her voice. "There are symbols here, invisible to the naked eye."

Ethan's skepticism melted away as he peered closely at the illuminated skulls. "Incredible," he murmured, awestruck by the discovery. He hastily retrieved a pad of paper from his pocket. "I'll draw them out, see how they look on paper."

The room was filled with the soft scratching of pen on paper, punctuated only by the steady rhythm of their breathing. Sofia traced the symbols with her finger, not yet knowing what they meant but excited all the same.

"Alright, I think I have them all," Ethan said finally, setting the pen aside as he and Sofia huddled together over the pad of paper. Their closeness sent a shiver down Sofia's spine, but she forced herself to concentrate on the symbols.

"Let's see if we can make sense of this," she said, her mind racing as she scanned the symbols, her expertise in linguistics guiding her through the translation process. As she worked, she was aware of Ethan's presence, his own knowledge of Mesoamerican languages providing invaluable assistance.

The minutes seemed to stretch into hours as they labored together, their minds working in tandem, unraveling the hidden message piece by piece. Finally, the last symbol fell into place, and the two leaned back, their eyes meeting in a mixture of triumph and trepidation.

"Is it...?" Sofia hesitated, hardly daring to voice the question that hung heavily in the air between them.

"We've done it," Ethan said, his voice tinged with both awe and apprehension. "Now we just need to understand what it means."

Ryan joined them, leaning over the paper. "Looks like a poem," he said. "A really dark, twisted poem."

The words seemed to echo in the small room, amplifying the tension that had been building since they began their translation. Sofia felt an unsettling familiarity with the writing.

Taking a deep breath, Sofia began to read the ancient words, their meaning unfolding with each passing syllable.

"Neteotl uan yectlehoilli; Huehueti cihuatli ticmati; Tlapalli uan eriliztli in xochitl mochipa huehuetiliztli; Auh teoaxcatlauhcayotl ye omeyolcuicatl; Teoyahualteopixqui in ticmati tlatzintlaolli; Yehuallachtihuiaya ic huitzocuepazque." She paused, pondering the words.

Ethan picked up where Sofia had left off. *"Lizaliz itech copa neteotl teohua, ica momac ilhuitlahtolcopa techcalpoloani manel t ictlaocoliztlaco chaneque-nepantlas neci-tlapaloaya inin yecticchihu, tlazocamati."*

The hairs on the back of Sofia's neck stood on end as the final word slipped from Ethan's lips. A chill ran down her spine as she considered the full implications of the poem's dark meaning.

"It's all Greek to me," Ryan said. "What does it mean?"

"It reminds me of some ancient curses I've seen on pyramids," Sofia said in a low voice, as if speaking too loudly would summon the darkness contained within the text. "In some cultures, they were etched into the very stones to protect the tombs from looters and desecrators."

Ethan glanced back at the calaveras, their hollow eye sockets appearing even more sinister under the black light's glow. He looked back at Sofia, concern etching lines across his forehead. "What exactly are you suggesting this is?"

She hesitated, her mind racing through the archives of knowledge she'd acquired over a lifetime of travel and study. The answer came to her like a cold whisper in the night, chilling her to the bone.

"I believe it's an old Aztec curse," she said softly, feeling the weight of her revelation. "One that requires a blood sacrifice in order to be lifted."

The silence in the evidence room was deafening, punctuated only by the hum of the black light and the distant sounds of the police station beyond the door. Sofia sensed the implication dawning on her companions like an oppressive fog.

"Then that must be what the killer is doing," Ethan whispered, his voice hoarse with dread. "He's trying to lift the curse by killing these people."

"Lift the curse," Ryan asked, "or bring on the curse?"

CHAPTER EIGHTEEN

Sofia's eyes darted back and forth from the computer screen to the pad of paper beside her as she typed out fragments of the Aztec poem. With every few lines, a chill ran through her, and she felt almost as if she were dealing with something better left undisturbed.

The smell of stale coffee and sweat hung heavily in the air of the police station, a constant reminder of the long hours spent working on cases that sometimes took months or even years to resolve. Ryan and Ethan stood behind her, silently watching as she entered the poem into a web browser.

This particular poem seemed to have an ominous feel to it; it spoke of lifting an evil curse through sacrifice, and Sofia couldn't shake the feeling that it had inspired their killer. She could almost hear the blood-curdling screams of the victims echoing in her ears, sending shivers down her spine.

Ryan Donovan's deep voice broke through her thoughts, startling her slightly. "Are you just trying to find any information you can on the poem?" he asked.

"Something like that," she said. "It's tricky, because it's not as if the poem has a title I can look up. I have to enter specific phrases and see what results I get."

She adjusted her search query, refining it to focus on the most obscure phrases within the poem. As she hit 'enter,' her heart raced in anticipation, hoping for a breakthrough.

Ethan leaned forward, pointing to a link that appeared near the top of the search results page. "What about this one?"

Sofia clicked on the link. It led to a blog that seemed to be dedicated to the study of Aztec culture, written by an archaeologist who had spent years digging into their history. A photograph of the blogger showed a middle-aged woman with short-cropped gray hair and wire-rimmed glasses perched on her nose. She wore khaki cargo pants and a dusty blue shirt, evidence of her time spent in the field.

"Interesting," Sofia muttered, scrolling through the blog entries. The archaeologist had written extensively about the poem in question, diving deep into its meaning and historical context. She claimed that the poem was a rare find, one that spoke of powerful rituals used by ancient shamans to lift curses placed upon their people. Yet, she also emphasized the importance of understanding these rituals within their cultural context, rather than taking them at face value.

"Could she be our killer?" Ryan asked, his voice filled with doubt.

Sofia studied the archaeologist's blog more closely, her dark eyes scanning the text for any hint of malicious intent. However, as she read between the lines, it became increasingly clear that this woman was not their killer. Her dedication to preserving the culture and history of the Aztecs was evident in every word she wrote. Moreover, her tone was filled with a genuine passion that Sofia felt would be difficult to fake.

"I don't think so," she said, her fingers hovering over the keyboard as she weighed her next move. "This woman is an academic; she wants to preserve history, not exploit it."

"Then we're back to square one," Ryan said, frustration creeping into his voice.

"Maybe not," Ethan said. "Try looking up a different line from the poem, something darker. Our killer seems to be drawn to the more sinister aspects of Aztec culture."

Sofia nodded, considering his suggestion. She glanced at the pad of paper next to her, picking out a particularly ominous phrase from the poem. As she entered the words into the search bar, she held her breath, hoping for a breakthrough.

The search engine churned out a handful of results, but one in particular caught Sofia's attention—a blog written by someone who lived in the San Francisco area. The title alone sent a shiver down her spine, and she hesitated for a moment before clicking on the link.

"Found something?" Ethan asked, leaning in closer to get a better look at the screen.

"Maybe," Sofia replied, her pulse quickening as she navigated to the blog.

The blog that appeared before Sofia was a stark contrast to the academic one they had just left. An eerie, blood-red background framed the black text on the page, with flickering shadows of what looked like sacrificial daggers dancing across the screen. The header read "Embracing the Darkness" in a jagged font, and the sidebar displayed various images of ancient Aztec rituals, some more unsettling than others.

"Looks like we've found ourselves a different kind of enthusiast," Ethan said, his voice low as if he feared disturbing the sinister ambiance that seemed to radiate from the computer monitor.

"Look at this." Ryan pointed to the blog's main content, filled with post after post, dedicated to the darker aspects of Aztec culture. Human sacrifices, bloodletting rituals, and supernatural curses were described in meticulous detail, accompanied by illustrations and photographs that made Sofia's stomach churn. It was clear that the author of the blog didn't just have an interest in these morbid aspects, but reveled in them.

"Whoever is behind this has a sick fascination with pain and death," she muttered, her fingers hovering above the keyboard as she fought the urge to slam the laptop shut and wipe its twisted contents from her mind. "This could be our guy."

"Check the bio," Ryan suggested.

With a growing sense of unease, Sofia clicked on the biography page, half expecting to find a manifesto declaring the blogger's intentions to carry out a series of ritualistic murders.

Instead, the biography page provided almost no information about the person behind the blog. There was no name, no photograph, no indication of where they lived or worked—only an unusual nickname: "Lord of Shadows." It was as if the blogger was deliberately concealing his identity, allowing his twisted obsession to speak for itself.

"Lord of Shadows," Sofia murmured, the nickname echoing in her mind like a chilling whisper. An idea sparked within her, and she turned away from the blog to open the police database on a separate window. Her fingers danced across the keyboard as she typed in the unusual moniker, her heart pounding in anticipation.

"Searching for the nickname?" Ethan asked.

"Exactly," Sofia replied, her eyes glued to the screen as the search results began to load. "If this person is using it as an alias, maybe we can find a connection."

As the search results came up, one entry caught Sofia's attention: a man named Brian Besser. She clicked on the file, and a photograph of a large, intimidating-looking man appeared. His face was hard, like chiseled stone, with a long scar running down his left cheek. He had close-cropped hair and cold, unfeeling eyes that seemed to bore into Sofia's very soul. There was no smile or hint of warmth in his expression—only a dark, unsettling presence that sent a shiver down her spine.

Beneath the photograph, Sofia found information about outstanding warrants against Besser. He was wanted for a string of violent crimes, including assault, kidnapping, and arson—all committed with a ritualistic flair that mirrored the Aztec practices detailed in the Lord of Shadows's blog.

As Ryan looked over her shoulder, his eyes widened at the sight of Besser's photograph and rap sheet.

"Seems you've struck gold," he murmured, his voice tinged with both admiration and unease. "We need to find him before he strikes again."

Sofia scrolled farther down the page until she found Besser's last known address. It was an old warehouse located in the industrial district—not exactly a place one would expect to find a history enthusiast, but then again, their suspect was nothing if not unconventional.

"Let's go," Sofia said, her voice resolute as she pushed back her chair and rose. "It's a long shot, but maybe we'll find something that can help us track him down."

Ethan gave her a bittersweet smile. "Wish I could tag along. But I should probably stay here and update the chief on what we discovered. Besides, I want to take another look at those skulls and make sure we didn't miss anything with that black light."

She nodded, trying to hide her disappointment. "Alright, then. Maybe we'll bump into you later?"

He grinned wryly. "One can hope."

Sofia smiled back, and she and Ryan moved away, hurrying down the corridor.

It was time to drag the Lord of Shadows back into the light.

CHAPTER NINETEEN

"Looks like a haunted house set up for Halloween," Sofia remarked as she and Ryan sat in her car, staring at the dilapidated structure before them. It was the last known residence of Brian Besser, but from the look of it, he was long gone.

The house stood in a poor part of town, surrounded by neglected properties and crumbling sidewalks. Its paint was long gone, leaving behind exposed wood that creaked with every gust of wind. A rusty chain-link fence surrounded the property, adding to the eerie atmosphere. The streetlights flickered weakly, casting bizarre shadows on the cracked pavement.

Sofia couldn't help but shudder as she took in the sight of the house. She had been to many places around the world and seen a multitude of cultures. Still, this particular scene sent a chill down her spine. It was as if the very air around the house was heavy with darkness and unspoken secrets.

"Seems fitting for our guy, doesn't it?" Ryan said, his voice breaking through her thoughts. "Seeing as how he styles himself the 'Lord of Shadows' and all? Maybe he's a vampire."

She glanced over at her partner, his blue eyes reflecting the dim light from the car's dashboard. There were the makings of a wry grin on his face.

"Well, that's too bad," Sofia said, "because I'm fresh out of garlic."

They got out of the vehicle and slowly approached the house. As they drew near, everything about the place suggested to Sofia that no one had been there in quite some time. The driveway was empty, void of any signs of recent tire tracks or footprints; several windows were broken, their jagged edges resembling sinister grins and the lawn, wild and untamed, was a chaotic mess of weeds and tall grass that seemed to reach out toward them as they walked past. The wind whispered through the overgrown foliage, creating a cacophony of rustling that only heightened the sense of unease that settled over Sofia.

Feeling a little silly, Sofia knocked on the front door. The sound of her knuckles meeting the weathered wood reverberated through the quiet night, unanswered. Ryan glanced around the desolate neighborhood, his eyes narrowing in thought.

"Maybe we should try to find any associates Besser might have had," he suggested, "and ask them where he is now."

Sofia, however, wasn't ready to leave just yet. Her gaze was drawn to a small garage next to the house, its door slightly ajar. An inexplicable pull urged her to investigate further. "I want to check out that garage first," she said, nodding toward it.

Ryan raised an eyebrow but didn't protest. Together, they approached the garage, their footsteps crunching over fallen leaves and debris. As they got closer, Sofia's heart raced in anticipation, her instincts telling her there was more to this place than met the eye.

The wind picked up, sending a shiver down Sofia's spine as she reached for the garage door. She paused, hearing a faint sound from within—something rustling, perhaps? Bracing herself, she gripped the edge of the door and yanked it open, revealing the dark interior.

A sudden flurry of movement caught her off guard, and she instinctively stepped back. It was only a wild animal, though—a scruffy-looking raccoon that had been rummaging through the trash inside the garage. With a chittering cry, it scurried past her feet and disappeared into the night.

"Damn," Sofia muttered, her pulse still racing from the surprise. She looked around the dimly lit space, trying to regain her bearings. The garage was cluttered with old boxes and broken furniture, a thick layer of dust covering every surface.

"Any sign of Besser?" Ryan asked, peering over her shoulder.

"Not unless he has the ability to shapeshift into a raccoon," Sofia replied, making no effort to hide her disappointment. She flicked on a light, illuminating the garage with a sickly yellow glow. The bare bulb hanging from the ceiling cast long shadows across the concrete floor, revealing the absence of any vehicle. Cobwebs hung like ghostly curtains in the corners, and a thick layer of dust covered everything, making it clear that no one had been here recently.

"Nothing," she said to Ryan as she stepped back out of the garage, shaking her head. "It looks like nobody's been here for a while."

"Damn," Ryan muttered, running a hand through his short blond hair. Ryan pulled out his phone, dialed a number, and then held the phone to his ear. "I'm going to see if I can reach the officer who last arrested Besser," he said.

Sofia nodded, but she found herself looking over Ryan's shoulder and across the street. A man was sitting on his porch, his eyes locked on them as he rocked gently in an old wooden chair. Intrigued, Sofia decided to approach him.

"Stay on the line," she told Ryan, then gestured toward the man on the porch. "I'm gonna go talk to him."

He nodded. "I'll follow you."

As Sofia walked across the street, her boots crunching the gravel, she couldn't help but wonder if the man had any connection to Besser or knew anything that could help them with their investigation. She could feel his piercing gaze following her every movement, and she tried to shake off the uneasy feeling that settled over her.

As Sofia neared the house, her eyes took in the faded paint on the clapboard siding and the unkempt lawn that surrounded it. The property was not in particularly great shape, but it looked as sharp as a Marine's bunk compared to Besser's rundown house.

The neighbor himself was a middle-aged man with a grizzled beard and eyes that appeared to have seen their fair share of hardship. He watched the agents approach, still rocking gently, showing neither friendliness nor hostility.

"Excuse me, sir," Sofia began as she neared the porch. "Do you happen to know Brian Besser, by any chance?"

The man's eyes flicked between the two agents, his expression guarded. "Who's asking?" he asked, leaning back in his rocker with a wary look.

"Special Agent Sofia Blake," she replied, flashing her badge. "This is my partner, Special Agent Ryan Donovan."

Ryan, who had continued to hold the phone to his ear as he followed Sofia, now lowered it, and shook his head regretfully. Apparently the officer wasn't picking up.

"Name's Pete," the man on the porch said cautiously, his grip tightening on the arms of his rocker. "I've seen Brian around. What do you want with him?"

Sofia exchanged a glance with Ryan before answering. "We're in the middle of an ongoing investigation, and Besser is a person of interest."

"Can't say I'm surprised," Pete replied, his voice tinged with disdain. "Brian's always getting into some kind of trouble. Devious sort of fellow, if you ask me."

Ryan raised an eyebrow, curiosity piqued. "What makes you say that?"

Pete leaned forward, casting a furtive glance toward the abandoned house across the street. "He's got a way of sliding into the shadows when things get hot. Never can tell what he's up to, but I've seen enough to know it's no good."

"Can you recall when you last saw Brian, Pete?" Sofia asked.

"Let me think... Must've been a couple weeks back," Pete mused, his eyes narrowing as he stared off into the distance. "Brian's sneaky, though. Comes around at night when he thinks nobody's watching."

"Interesting," Sofia murmured, her dark hair whipping around her face in the cool November breeze.

"Do you happen to know what kind of vehicle Brian drives?" Ryan asked.

"Sure do," Pete replied, nodding slowly. "It's a beat-up old pickup truck, dark blue. Can't miss it."

"Any idea why he's been coming back?" Ryan asked. "The house looks abandoned."

Pete shook his head. "It was foreclosed, last I knew. I thought about telling the bank he's still coming around, but...well...I don't like prying into others' business, know what I mean?"

Sofia resisted the urge to smile. She found it rather amusing that a man who made a habit of tracking his neighbor's movements should talk about respecting others' privacy.

"Well, we appreciate the information," Ryan said. "Here's my card in case he shows up again."

As Ryan handed his card to Pete, Sofia's gaze drifted upward to the corner of Pete's house. A small security camera perched there caught her attention.

"Pete," she said, "I couldn't help but notice your security camera. Why did you install it if you don't mind my asking?"

"Truth be told, ever since Brian moved in across the street, I've had my suspicions about him," Pete admitted, shifting uncomfortably in his rocker. "Figured I'd keep an eye on things, just in case."

"Would you mind if we checked the footage from the night you last saw Brian?" Sofia asked, her heart pounding with anticipation.

"Of course," Pete agreed, standing up from his rocking chair with a slight grimace. "Come on in, and I'll show you."

Sofia and Ryan followed Pete into his modest home, the floorboards creaking beneath her footsteps. The air inside was warm and slightly musty, the scent of aging wood and worn furniture mingling with the faint aroma of coffee.

"Computer's in the living room," Pete said, leading them through a dimly lit corridor adorned with family photos and framed newspaper clippings. "Should have the footage you're looking for there."

Sofia stepped into the living room, the muted light from an old table lamp casting shadows across the worn carpet. A calico cat with piercing green eyes lounged on a maroon armchair, its gaze following her cautiously. The room was filled with mismatched furniture and knick-knacks that seemed to hold sentimental value rather than monetary worth. Family photos lined the walls, their faces frozen in time.

"Make yourselves comfortable," Pete said, gesturing toward the armchair opposite the cat. "I'll bring up the footage."

While Ryan settled into the chair, Sofia found herself examining the room more closely, her curiosity piqued. There was something about this house that spoke of a life lived in quiet resilience, a testament to the man who called it home. Her eyes drifted over the various trinkets and mementos, each telling a story of their own. She found herself drawn to a small collection of foreign coins, reminders of her own extensive travels.

"Here we go," Pete announced, interrupting her thoughts as he brought up the security footage on his dusty computer screen. Sofia and Ryan leaned in, studying the grainy images intently.

The video showed Besser's vehicle pulling up to his abandoned-looking house late at night. His headlights illuminated the unkempt lawn for a brief moment before he switched them off and drove around to the back of the house, disappearing from view.

"Any idea what he was doing back there?" Sofia asked.

Pete shook his head, his eyes narrowed in thought. "Not sure. Going in the back door, I'd guess, but why he'd want to go into that derelict house in the first place is beyond me."

"Could you rewind and freeze on the vehicle when I say so?" Ryan replied, his gaze still fixed on the screen.

Pete rewound, then paused at Ryan's instruction. Ryan jotted down Besser's license plate number and dialed a number on his phone, speaking in hushed tones as he put out an APB on Besser's vehicle. Sofia turned to Pete.

"Thank you, Pete," she said. "You've been incredibly helpful."

"Anything I can do to help catch that man," he replied. "He's a bad apple, through and through."

As they stepped back outside, the chill November air enveloped them like an icy embrace. Sofia shivered involuntarily, more from the sinister atmosphere than the cold, as she and Ryan crossed the street and returned to her car.

"I still don't get it," she mused. "Why does Besser keep coming back to this place? What is he hiding?"

"Maybe he's taking his victims here," Ryan suggested grimly, his eyes searching the darkened windows of the abandoned-looking house. "It would certainly be secluded enough."

Sofia bit her lip, considering the possibility. "We need to search the place, see if there's any evidence to support that theory," she said, feeling a growing sense of urgency.

"Agreed, but we'll need a search warrant first." Ryan glanced at his watch. "And it's late. We'll have to wait until tomorrow."

"Every minute we wait is another minute Besser could be hurting someone," Sofia murmured, her fingers curling into fists at her side. The thought stirred a deep anger within her, fueling her determination to bring him to justice.

Ryan placed a comforting hand on her shoulder. "Trust me, I know. But we have to do this by the book. It's the only way to make sure he doesn't slip through the cracks again."

Sofia nodded. She knew Ryan was right—they couldn't afford any missteps. But as she gazed at the shadowy silhouette of the house, she couldn't help but feel that time was running out, and that somewhere within those darkened walls, the answers they so desperately sought might be waiting to be discovered.

The sudden ringing of Ryan's phone cut through the silence like a knife. His hand shot into his pocket, quickly pulling out the device. As he answered the call, his expression shifted, eyes widening, brow furrowing with concern.

"Got it. Thanks for the update." He ended the call and turned to Sofia, urgency etched across his face. "That was the station. They got a hit on Besser's license plate. It's parked in a lot near the festival in La Porta."

"He's hunting," she said, hurriedly climbing back into the car and starting the engine. "But he's about to find out he isn't at the top of the food chain."

CHAPTER TWENTY

"You think he's stalking someone right now?" Ryan said in a low voice as he and Sofia studied the crowd of revelers in downtown La Porta.

Sofia's eyes flitted from face to face, profiling and categorizing. She wanted to believe that she would know the killer when she saw him, but the truth was that serial killers didn't have some distinct look or way of moving that set them apart. They were just like everyone else, which made their presence even more unsettling.

"I hope so," she said. "Because if he is, that means we're not too late."

She was distracted by the sight of a police cruiser cutting through the sea of revelers, its headlights casting eerie shadows on the skeletal decorations that lined the streets. It glided to a stop beside Sofia's vehicle, and an officer stepped out.

He was a tall man with a muscular build, his uniform immaculate despite the dusty environment. His eyes were sharp, and he carried himself with a confidence that made it clear he'd been on the force for years.

"Special Agent Blake?" he asked, addressing Sofia. "I'm Officer Martinez. Got your message about Besser's vehicle."

"Nice to meet you, Officer Martinez," Sofia replied, shaking his proffered hand. Ryan did the same, introducing himself.

"Thanks for getting here so quickly," Ryan said.

"Of course. My partner's keeping an eye on the suspect's vehicle in case he decides to get out of Dodge. I'll take you there."

Sofia's heart pounded in her chest as she walked through the throngs of festivalgoers, following Officer Martinez. The scent of marigolds and incense filled the air, mingling with the aroma of street food cooking nearby. Once again she found her eyes darting from face to face, searching for any hint that Besser might be among them. Her fingers twitched with the anticipation of reaching for her gun, ready at a moment's notice.

As they navigated the narrow paths between stalls selling brightly colored trinkets and food stands offering spicy treats, Sofia began to feel exposed. She and Ryan were dressed casually, blending in with the crowd, but Officer Martinez's uniform stood out like a beacon. If Besser spotted them together, he would know without a doubt that something was amiss.

Nothing to be done about it now, she thought. *Let's just hope he doesn't look our way.*

Finally, they reached a quieter area of the festival where fewer people milled about, allowing Sofia to breathe a little easier. Officer Martinez gestured toward a man leaning against a wall, his eyes locked on a car parked across the street.

"There's my partner, Officer Coleman," he said.

Officer Coleman was a shorter man, his dark hair flecked with gray. A seasoned officer, no doubt. He had positioned himself behind a vendor's cart selling sugar skull candies, using it as cover while he kept watch on the unassuming pickup parked nearby.

The truck itself was an older model, its once-vibrant blue paint now dulled by age and neglect. It was the perfect vehicle for someone trying to blend in, not drawing any attention to themselves.

Officer Martinez led Sofia and Ryan over to his partner.

"I've been watching the suspect's vehicle since we spotted it," Coleman said by way of greeting. "No sign of him yet."

"Thanks, Officer Coleman," Sofia replied. "We appreciate your help."

Sofia's eyes narrowed as she scanned the bustling crowd, her instincts on high alert. The air was thick with the scent of frying churros and carne asada, mingling with the smoky aroma of copal incense. She could feel the bass of the music pounding in her chest, echoing the rapid rhythm of her heartbeat.

"Any idea where Besser might be?" she asked Coleman.

Coleman shook his head, his expression grim. "No idea. Could be anywhere, as far as I know."

A shiver of unease snaked down Sofia's spine, her mind racing with dark possibilities. She couldn't shake the nagging feeling that something wasn't right. What if Besser had spotted Coleman watching the vehicle and decided to flee? He could be long gone already, and they'd be wasting their time watching his truck.

"You guys can head back to your duties," Ryan said to the officers. "We'll take it from here."

"Are you sure, Agent Donovan?" Martinez asked, concern etched on his face. "We can stick around a while longer if you need us."

"Thanks, but we've got it covered," Ryan said, offering the officers a reassuring smile. "Appreciate your help."

"Good luck," Coleman said, raising a hand in farewell before he and Martinez disappeared into the throngs of revelers.

The cacophony of laughter and music from the Día de los Muertos festival drowned out the hum of anxious thoughts in Sofia's mind as her eyes darted from Besser's truck to the festivalgoers.

Ryan, ever vigilant beside her, broke the silence between them. "You know, there's a food truck over there," he said, nodding toward a brightly painted vehicle nearby. "We might as well eat while we wait—no telling how long it'll be before Besser shows up. Want anything?"

Sofia hesitated, considering his words. Before she could answer, however, her attention was suddenly drawn to a figure emerging from the shadows. Her heart skipped a beat as she realized the man's features matched the description they had of Besser.

"Ryan," she whispered urgently, her voice barely audible above the din around them. "Look."

He followed her gaze, his own eyes narrowing as he took in the sight of their target approaching the vehicle.

Without missing a beat, the two agents emerged from their hiding place and began to close in on Besser. As they neared him, the man froze, sensing their presence. His eyes darted between Sofia and Ryan, panic clouding his face as he realized he'd been discovered.

"Brian Besser?" Sofia called.

He remained fixed in place, rooted to the spot.

Don't do it, Sofia thought. *Don't you dare—*

In an instant, he turned on his heel and sprinted back the way he came.

"Damn it!" Ryan cursed, surging forward in pursuit. Sofia matched his pace, her every muscle straining as they raced after their quarry.

Besser soon disappeared into the crowd. Sofia and Ryan plunged in after him, weaving through the throng of people. The vibrant colors of the Día de los Muertos celebration swirled around them in a dizzying blur, while the scent of street food and burning incense mingled in the air.

"Watch out!" Ryan shouted, his deep voice cutting through the cacophony as he shouldered between two men.

Sofia felt the edge of a vendor's cart graze her side, but she refused to let it slow her down. Her breath came in ragged gasps, her chest heaving as adrenaline coursed through her veins. She cursed inwardly, knowing that if only they had approached Besser differently, they might already have him in custody. But dwelling on the past wouldn't help them now; what mattered was catching him before he vanished into the night.

"Where did he go?" Ryan asked, pulling up to scan the crowd.

"Over there!" Sofia cried, spotting Besser as he climbed over a wooden fence. They sprinted toward it, their shoes pounding against the packed dirt of the street.

It was a cattle enclosure, empty except for a large, mean-looking bull that roused itself as Besser pelted across the mud. It appeared Besser would probably reach the fence at the far side before the bull reached him, but if Sofia or Ryan went in after him, they might not be so lucky.

"Damn it!" Ryan growled, frustration etching lines across his face. "We'll have to go around."

Sofia, however, didn't follow Ryan as he ran around the enclosure. The fence butted up against the side of a large pavilion, so it appeared it would take some time to detour all the way around. Sofia wasn't willing to do so, not if it meant Besser might escape.

Instead she vaulted into the pen. The bull immediately turned its attention to her, its horns glinting menacingly in the dim light. Its eyes seemed to bore into her soul, full of rage and power, daring her to make a move. For a brief moment, she hesitated, weighing the risk against the need to apprehend Besser.

"Come on, Sofia," she murmured under her breath, steeling herself. "You can do this."

With a burst of speed, she darted to her left, narrowly avoiding the bull's charge. Its horns grazed her side, tearing a hole in her jacket, but leaving her otherwise unscathed. She stumbled over uneven ground, her eyes never leaving Besser as he clambered over the fence separating the pen from another enclosure.

Almost there, she thought, her focus singular as she sprinted toward the fence. The bull snorted behind her, its hooves thundering against the ground as it gave chase.

As Sofia reached the barrier, she leaped onto it, her fingers grasping at the rough wood just as the bull lunged for her once more. The force of its impact rattled the fence beneath her, but she held on with grim determination, hauling herself over the top.

Sofia panted as she slid down into the second enclosure. Her shoes sank into the mud, slowing her progress.

Ahead, Besser raced across the muddy expanse, casting frantic glances back at his pursuer. The fear in his eyes only fueled Sofia's resolve—she couldn't let him reach the crowd on the far side and disappear again.

Ryan won't make it in time, she thought, noting the absence of her partner as she scanned the fence line. *It's up to me.*

Her breaths came in ragged gasps, her lungs burning with exertion as she sprinted across the muddy pen. The squelching of her shoes in the muck was nearly drowned out by the pounding of her heart. She could almost taste victory as the distance between her and Besser rapidly closed. The fence loomed before them, a final obstacle standing between Sofia and the justice she sought.

Almost...there... she thought, her mind locked onto her target. Her legs felt like they were made of lead, but she couldn't afford to slow down now.

Besser threw his weight against the fence, scrambling desperately to climb it. His grip slipped on the slick wood, opening the window of opportunity Sofia needed. Mustering the last of her strength, she launched herself forward, her fingers closing around his ankle just as he began to clear the top.

Bracing herself as well as she could, she gave his leg a hard yank. His eyes widened in shock and fear as he plummeted, landing hard on his back in the mud with a resounding thud.

Ryan's footsteps pounded across the hard-packed ground as he raced up to the far side of the fence just a few moments later. "Nice work," he said, leaning on his knees as he caught his breath. "You got him."

"Damn right I did," Sofia said as she pulled out her handcuffs.

CHAPTER TWENTY ONE

"This is harassment," Besser said, his voice cold and defiant. "I haven't done anything wrong."

As Sofia stared at Besser across the table of the La Porta police station's interview room, she couldn't shake the feeling that there was something inherently violent about this man. It wasn't just his intimidating stature or the way he clenched his fists; it was the aura of cruelty that seemed to surround him like a cloud of smoke. She had encountered many dangerous individuals in her career, but few who made her blood run cold like Besser did.

In her gut, she sensed he was more than capable of murder.

The room was small, the walls painted a sterile white that only added to the suffocating atmosphere. A single window, barred and covered with a thick layer of grime, let in just a sliver of moonlight. The table and chairs were bolted to the floor, and an old, flickering light dangled precariously from the ceiling.

Besser sat hunched over in one of the chairs, still spattered with mud from his fall in the bull pen earlier. The agents had given him some paper towels to clean up, but he looked far from presentable. He needed a shower and a change of clothes, neither of which would be provided here.

Sofia took a deep breath, preparing herself for what was shaping up to be an adversarial interrogation.

"Actually, we have good reason to detain you," she said. "But we'll get to that. Why don't we start with why you ran away from us in the parking lot?"

"Odd thing for an innocent man to do," Ryan remarked as he leaned against the wall.

Besser shifted uncomfortably in his seat, avoiding eye contact. "I thought you were going to mug me, okay? It was dark, and I saw two people coming toward me. What would you have done?"

Ryan scoffed, crossing his arms over his broad chest. "Cut the crap, Besser. We're not buying it."

"Look," Besser insisted, raising his head defiantly. "I didn't do anything wrong. I'm just here for the festival, like everyone else."

"Speaking of which," Sofia interjected, leaning forward, and clasping her hands on the table. "We came across your blog. You seem to have quite a fascination with Aztec culture. I'm curious; what drew you to them?"

Besser's eyes lit up, suddenly dropping his guard. "Ah, yes. My interest in the Aztecs started when I was a teenager. I stumbled upon a book about their history at the library and was instantly captivated. Their power, their brutality—it's unlike anything else in history."

As Besser spoke, Sofia took note of the passion in his voice, the gleam in his eyes. It was clear that he was enamored with the Aztecs, but was it enough to drive him to commit murder?

And why is he so open about it? Sofia wondered. *If he's our guy, then it would make more sense for him to downplay his interest in the Aztecs—or, better yet, deny it altogether. Or does he think he simply can't be caught?*

"Power and brutality, huh?" Ryan remarked skeptically. "That seems to be a common thread these days. But why the Aztecs, specifically?"

"Because they were unapologetic in their conquests," Besser replied, his voice growing more animated by the second. "They were feared and respected. And their rituals, their connection to death—it was raw and primal. I've always been drawn to that."

Sofia's mind raced, attempting to piece together the puzzle that was Besser. His fascination with the Aztecs could be harmless, but it could also be a key component in understanding his potential involvement in the murders.

Her gaze fell on Besser's exposed arms, where a myriad of Aztec-themed tattoos snaked and intertwined along his sinewy flesh. Intricate symbols danced around the powerful image of Huitzilopochtli, the Aztec god of war, his obsidian blade poised to strike at any moment.

"Your tattoos," she began, her words slow and measured. "Tell me about them."

Besser glanced down at his inked skin, a glimmer of pride flickering in his eyes. He traced his fingers over the tattoos as if they were precious artifacts. "This one," he said, pointing to a fierce-looking jaguar, "represents Tepeyollotl, the god of earthquakes and echoes. And this—" he twisted his wrist to reveal a glyph etched into his forearm "—is the symbol for Tlaloc, the god of rain and fertility."

As Besser spoke, Sofia studied him closely, noting the way he seemed to wear his fascination with Aztec culture like a badge of honor. It was clear that he held no reservations about displaying his interests, but did that obsession extend to more sinister acts? Was he truly capable of murder?

"Interesting," she murmured, filing away the information for future reference. Yet, something nagged at her—a vital piece of the puzzle that remained elusive. She needed to test the depths of Besser's knowledge further.

"*¿Tlen tikmatiske in tlahtolli?*" she asked in fluent Nahuatl, her voice smooth and controlled as she asked whether he was familiar with Nahuatl. She watched Besser intently, searching for any hint of recognition or understanding.

His brow furrowed, eyes filling with confusion. "What?"

She repeated the question again, enunciating each syllable carefully.

"Uh, I don't know what you're saying," Besser admitted, his expression a mix of bewilderment and frustration. "What language is that?"

Sofia couldn't help but feel a flicker of disappointment at Besser's apparent lack of knowledge regarding the very culture he claimed to admire. Nevertheless, she filed away this information as potentially important.

"It's Nahuatl," she replied, her tone neutral. "The language of the Aztecs."

"Ah," he muttered, avoiding eye contact. "I never really got around to learning it."

Sofia leaned back in her chair, her thoughts racing. Was Besser's ignorance a sign of innocence, or was it simply another layer of deception?

"I'm surprised," she said. "For someone so fascinated with the Aztecs, I'd have thought you would've tried to learn their language."

Besser shifted in his seat, his muddy clothes sticking to his skin. He sighed, running a hand through his unkempt hair. "Languages were never my strong suit," he admitted, his gaze darting around the room as if searching for an escape. "I tried learning some basics, but it just didn't stick."

Sofia narrowed her eyes, trying to discern whether Besser was being truthful or simply playing dumb. His body language seemed genuine, but there was something about his demeanor that left her feeling unsettled.

As Sofia weighed her doubts, Ryan leaned forward, his eyes boring into Besser. "Alright, let's change gears for a moment. Where were you this afternoon?"

"Here in La Porta," Besser replied without hesitation. "At the festival, all day." He relaxed slightly, his voice taking on a hint of enthusiasm as he described the vibrant colors and lively atmosphere of the festival. "It's amazing, really. The whole town comes alive to celebrate death. The parades, the music, the people dressed as skeletons dancing through the streets—it's like something out of a dream."

Sofia listened carefully, observing the way Besser's eyes lit up as he spoke of the celebration. "Alright," she said slowly, shifting her weight from one foot to the other. "You've told us about this afternoon, but what about last night? Where were you then?"

"Last night?" Besser hesitated, a bead of sweat forming on his brow. "I was sleeping in my car."

Again, no alibi, Sofia thought.

"Why do you keep returning to your house if you're living out of your car? " she asked. "And why are you so secretive about it? The place looks abandoned."

Besser shifted uncomfortably in his seat, clenching and unclenching his fists as if trying to find the right words. "I sleep in my car most of the time, but sometimes I go back to work on projects in my basement. I have to be discreet because the house is foreclosed."

Sofia's eyes narrowed, her instincts telling her that there was more to the story than Besser was letting on. She glanced at Ryan, who seemed equally unconvinced by Besser's explanation.

"Come on," Ryan said. "You expect us to believe that?"

Besser glared at Ryan. "It's the truth. What do you think I'm doing in there, sacrificing cats?"

His words caused gooseflesh to stand on Sofia's arms. *Not cats,* she thought darkly. *Something far worse.*

As much as she would have liked to keep grilling Besser, she needed to take a step back and process what they'd learned so far. She rose, clearing her throat.

"Sit tight, Mr. Besser," she said. "We'll be back." With that, she strode out of the interview room, Ryan following closely behind.

Once they were alone in the dimly lit hallway, Ryan turned to Sofia, his expression grim. "He's lying, Sofia. We need to keep pressuring him until he cracks."

"Perhaps," Sofia replied. She couldn't shake the feeling that they were missing some crucial piece of information. "While you do that, I'm going to head to the evidence room and take another look at those calaveras. There has to be something we're overlooking."

Ryan nodded slowly, his features grim. "You think the killer's still out there?"

"I think we have to be prepared for the possibility. Because if the killer's still free, I want to figure that out on my own—not by learning he's killed someone else."

CHAPTER TWENTY TWO

Sofia's brow furrowed as she leaned closer to the two calaveras, the dim light casting eerie shadows on the stainless steel table.

There must be something I'm missing, she thought.

The evidence room felt colder than it had before, the sterile air nipping at her exposed skin, making her shiver involuntarily. It was late, but she knew sleep wouldn't come easy tonight, not when there was still so much work to be done.

A pad of paper lay beside the calaveras, covered in scribbles and translations that she and Ethan had painstakingly decoded from the mysterious symbols etched into the ancient skulls. Her eyes darted back and forth between the pad and the calaveras, double-checking each symbol for accuracy.

Her heart raced with anticipation, hoping that perhaps they had missed a crucial element that would help them solve this twisted case. But as she came to the end of the list, she sighed in defeat. Everything seemed to be exactly as she and Ethan had initially determined, at least concerning the symbols visible to the naked eye.

Still holding onto a thread of hope, she reached up and switched off the overhead lights, plunging the room into darkness. She hesitated for a moment, listening to the sound of her own breathing, before flicking on a black light. The room transformed, bathed in an eerie purple glow that made the calaveras appear even more sinister than before—if that were possible.

Sofia moved methodically, examining every inch of the skulls under the black light, searching for anything that might've been hidden or overlooked. As she worked, her mind wandered to Ethan. She admired his lithe, athletic form and how his dark hair seemed to effortlessly fall across his forehead, a look that was both dashing and boyish at the same time.

"Come on, there has to be something," she whispered to herself, her desperation mounting with every passing second. But as she completed her examination, the truth became painfully clear: there was nothing new here.

She stepped back, the weight of failure heavy on her chest. Curious to know how late it was getting, she pulled her phone from her pocket.

It was not the clock that drew her attention, however, but rather a message from her father, Emilio, asking about her progress with the translation of the calavera symbols.

"Maybe Dad can see something I can't," she murmured, hope igniting within her once more. She dialed his number, and after a couple of rings, his warm voice filled her ear.

"Hey, mija. How's it going? Did you find anything new?"

"Well, we did find some additional symbols on the skulls," Sofia began, her words tumbling out in a rush. "We used a black light and discovered more markings in invisible ink."

"Fascinating," Emilio murmured.

"Putting all the symbols together, we were able to translate them into a poem...but it's confusing."

"Tell me about it," Emilio said, sounding intrigued.

"It talks about human sacrifice and an ancient curse," Sofia explained. "But the way it's written...it's so vague. I can't tell if the poem is about lifting the curse or causing one."

Emilio went quiet for a moment, digesting the information. Sofia could practically hear him scratching his beard—a habit he had when deep in thought. She clenched her fists, waiting for any spark of insight he might offer.

"Can you send me the poem, Sofia?" he asked. "Maybe I can help you make sense of it."

"Of course," Sofia replied, her fingers tapping hurriedly on the screen as she sent him a picture of the translated poem. The silence between them grew heavy as Emilio studied the text.

"Interesting," he finally murmured, his voice distant and contemplative. "I see what you mean about it being vague. But don't worry, mija. We'll figure this out together. Remember that time we solved that ancient Sumerian riddle? This is no different."

A small smile tugged at the corners of Sofia's lips, recalling the memory of working late into the night with her father, surrounded by stacks of dusty books and cups of cooling coffee. It had been one of the highlights of her childhood—a bonding moment that had solidified their shared love for linguistics.

"Thanks, Dad," she said, her voice now steadier, soothed by his unwavering faith in her abilities.

Emilio cleared his throat. "You know, Sof, some of these words are palindromes."

She was silent for a few seconds as she studied the poem. Then the words jumped out at her, reading the same backwards as forwards, just as her father had said.

"Of course!" She could barely exclaim her excitement.

"Now," Emilio was saying, "if you separate the palindromes..."

Sofia was already on it, however, writing the palindromes on a separate sheet of paper. Then she chewed on the end of the pen as she studied the symbols.

The once-jumbled mess of letters had transformed into a chilling message: "Four victims lift the curse." A shiver ran down Sofia's spine as she read the words aloud.

"Four victims," Emilio echoed, his voice heavy. "How many has he taken so far?"

"Three," Sofia said. "That means—"

"He's only got one left," her father finished for her. "And if he's timing these sacrifices with Día de los Muertos—"

"Then that means he *has* to take another victim within the next twenty-four hours." Sofia swallowed hard. "Because if he doesn't, all his work will have been for nothing."

CHAPTER TWENTY THREE

Sofia tightened her jacket around her shoulders as she walked slowly down the street, her expert eyes scanning the dwindling crowd for any sign of suspicious activity.

Somewhere out here, she thought, the killer was on the hunt, and he would not stop until he had his final prize.

A crisp Californian breeze rustled through the paper marigolds and skeletal decorations that adorned the makeshift altars. The scent of incense mingled with the sweet aroma of pan de muerto and tamales, creating an intoxicating blend that seemed to hang heavy in the air. Despite the beauty and splendor of the festivities, Sofia couldn't shake the feeling of dread that had settled in her chest.

As she continued her search, she noticed a young woman standing by one of the altars, her face pale, and hands trembling. She looked lost, like a fragile bird caught in a storm. Her large, doe-like eyes darted nervously around the square.

It occurred to Sofia that all the killer's victims thus far had been vulnerable young women, just like this one. A sudden inspiration struck her.

Maybe if I make myself vulnerable enough, she thought, *he'll come after me.*

Ryan had sent out a warning about the killer's activities, but it didn't seem anything had really changed, which suggested to Sofia that the killer was probably still here. If she could become the prey, maybe she could catch the predator before he struck again.

Her eyes scanned the remaining festival goers as she walked, her gaze lingering on a woman who was packing up her small clothing stall. The vendor was middle-aged with short, graying hair and deep lines etched into her face, signs of a life spent outdoors in the sun. Her hands, roughened by years of labor, deftly folded the clothes she had been selling earlier in the day. The stall was a riot of colors, offering traditional dresses, scarves, and embroidered blouses that still hung from the wooden racks.

"Excuse me," Sofia said, approaching the woman. "I know it's late, but would you mind if I quickly picked out a few things?"

The woman looked up, her eyes narrowing as she assessed Sofia. "No, I'm sorry. It's too late. I'm closing up for the night."

"Please," Sofia implored, holding out a handful of cash. "I'll pay extra, and I promise to be quick about it."

The vendor hesitated, her gaze flicking between Sofia's face and the money in her hand. Finally, with a sigh, she nodded. "Alright, but make it fast."

"Thank you," Sofia said, quickly scanning the array of clothing before her.

She needed something that would make her look vulnerable, like easy prey to lure the killer out. Sofia chose a white lace dress with long sleeves, its delicate fabric giving off an air of innocence. She also picked out a soft, light shawl that she could drape over her shoulders, leaving her neck exposed. To complete the look, she selected a pair of flat sandals adorned with small, colorful beads. They'd make her appear less imposing than the boots she currently wore.

"These will do nicely," she said, presenting her selections to the vendor.

The woman nodded, taking the clothes, and folding them with practiced efficiency. Sofia handed over the cash and thanked the woman once more before slipping away to find a secluded spot to change. The thought of making herself look vulnerable, like the killer's previous victims, sent a shiver down her spine. But she knew it was necessary if she wanted to catch him.

She slipped into a dark alley, the shadows swallowing her up as she stepped away from the festive lights still clinging to the buildings. The narrow passageway reeked of dampness and decay, with crumbling bricks and discarded trash lining her path.

As she began to change, she noticed how the lively music and laughter of the festival had all but faded away, leaving only the distant echo of footsteps on cobblestones.

Is this really the best plan? she wondered, her fingers fumbling with the delicate fabric of the dress. She couldn't shake the feeling that she was putting herself in serious danger by transforming into the killer's ideal target. But then again, perhaps it was the best way to prevent him from harming anyone else. With that thought, she steeled herself and continued changing, the cold air raising goosebumps on her exposed flesh.

Once she was fully dressed in her new attire, she slipped her jacket back on to keep herself warm. Then she took a moment to try to conceal the gun. No matter how she shifted it, however, she couldn't seem to conceal the weapon, not without a specialized holster.

She stared at the weapon, debating what to do. If the killer saw she was carrying a gun, he would very quickly realize she wasn't such an easy target. If, on the other hand, she left the gun behind, there was no telling what might happen to her.

"Oh, what the hell," she finally muttered, slipping the weapon into the bundle of her old clothes. Then she stuck the whole pile behind a dumpster, leaving it on a clean piece of cardboard.

As she stepped back out onto the street, the eerie silence wrapped around her like a blanket. Her heart pounded in her chest, each beat an urgent reminder of the dangerous game she'd begun to play. Her thoughts raced, wondering if she would be able to lure the killer into revealing himself.

"Keep it together, Sofia," she murmured under her breath, forcing her legs to move forward. "You've faced worse situations than this."

She tried to focus on the ghostly moonlight glinting off the dew-covered cobblestones, or the faint scent of marigolds carried by the breeze, anything to distract her from the gnawing unease that threatened to overwhelm her. She knew she had to be strong; lives were at stake.

"Stay focused," she whispered, her breath coming out in a soft cloud against the cool night air. "You can do this."

She moved down the street, the sound of her footsteps punctuating the silence that had fallen over La Porta. With each step she took, she could feel the darkness creeping in around her, enveloping her like a sinister cloak. Her chest tightened as she realized just how deserted the town had become, and she fought to suppress the shiver running down her spine.

"Showtime," she whispered to herself, forcing her posture into a deliberate slouch. She wanted to appear vulnerable, an easy target—the perfect bait for the killer. Running her fingers through her tousled locks, she allowed them to fall over her face, partially hiding her features. After a moment of hesitation, she removed her jacket and tossed it aside, leaving her arms exposed to the chilly night air. The goosebumps that erupted across her skin only added to her desired image of vulnerability.

She chose an open area near the center of the festival grounds, where the murderer would have ample opportunity to observe her from the shadows. She stood there, alone, feeling the weight of her solitude pressing down on her. Her senses were heightened, ears straining to catch any hint of movement. Her eyes darted back and forth, scanning the dark corners and hidden crevices surrounding her, searching for the lurking danger she knew was there.

I should let Ryan know where I am, she thought, pulling out her phone and dialing his number. The call rang through to voicemail, unanswered. Frustration flared inside her, but she quickly tempered it with a sigh. She realized he was probably still questioning Besser.

As the minutes wore on, Sofia began to be plagued by doubt. Maybe this hadn't been such a great idea. After all, there was no telling when, or if, the killer would find her. For all she knew, he could be miles away, having already snatched his next victim.

She decided it was time to abandon this risky plan. She needed to retrieve her old clothes and regroup with Ryan. Turning on her heel, she started to retrace her steps.

That was when she noticed him—a figure in the distance, cloaked in shadows. Her heart thudded in her chest, adrenaline coursing through her veins as she tried to determine whether he was just another festivalgoer or, perhaps, the predator she sought.

Stay calm, she told herself, continuing to walk at a steady pace, her thoughts racing faster than her steps. *You're a trained agent. You can handle this.*

With calculated precision, she veered off the main street and slipped into a dark alley. The narrow passage was shrouded in shadows, the perfect place to lay her ambush. As she moved farther in, the cacophony of the festival faded, replaced by the sounds of her own heartbeat and the distant scuffling of rats.

A dented dumpster sat against one wall, its lid slightly ajar, while an old fire escape cast a pattern of angular lines on the uneven pavement below. Sofia committed these details to memory, planning her attack with the same meticulousness she applied to everything else in her life.

Come on, she thought, willing the man to follow her into the darkness. *I'm ready for you.*

Her breath came in short, controlled bursts as she crouched behind the dumpster, ensuring that she could still see the opening of the alley. She reached for her weapon, but of course it was gone—she'd left it with her clothes, after all. It seemed she would have to rely on her wits and her fists.

Peering around the side of the dumpster, she watched the entrance of the alley with hawk-like focus, waiting for any sign of movement. Her heart pounded in her ears, drowning out all other sounds.

Come on. Where are you?

Finally the figure appeared at the entrance, hesitating for a moment before stepping cautiously into the darkness. The only problem was, he wasn't alone.

There were two other men with him.

CHAPTER TWENTY FOUR

Three? Sofia wondered, her unease deepening.

Her eyes narrowed as she studied the three men. She couldn't see much of them, not in the darkness of the alley, except that they moved with an easy, fluid grace. They seemed confident, as if they were in their natural element.

Her brows furrowed. She had believed that the killer was acting alone, so who were these three men? Were they accomplices, or did these three men have nothing to do with the murders?

Best to let them go on by, she thought, acutely aware of the danger she had put herself in. Nobody – not Ryan, not her father, not the police – knew where she was, so if anything went wrong, there wouldn't be anyone to come help her.

She pressed herself against the cold brick wall, praying that the shadows would cloak her from view. Her breaths came in short, sharp gasps, her chest heaving with the strain of her pounding heart. As the three men approached, she steeled herself, determined to remain undetected and glean as much information from their conversation as possible.

She could feel her palms sweating and her pulse racing at the prospect of being discovered. It seemed like an eternity before they were finally close enough to her hiding spot. Sofia held her breath, hoping it would be enough to muffle the sound in her ears.

That's when it happened; one of the men turned on a flashlight, sweeping its beam through the darkness. The light found her, illuminating her face like a spotlight on a stage. She cursed inwardly, knowing she'd been caught.

"Aw, look what we have here." The man laughed, his voice dripping with malice. "Looks like someone wants to play a little game with us."

Sofia knew there was no point in continuing to hide. Taking a deep breath, she stepped out from her concealed position and faced the trio head-on. "I'm with the FBI. Turn around and go back where you came from." Her voice was steady, betraying none of the fear that churned inside her.

As she studied each of them, she noted their features: One was tall and lanky with a crooked nose, another had short, stocky legs and a bushy beard, while the third man – the one who had first noticed her – had a scar running down one side of his face, a permanent sneer etched into his skin.

The bearded man let out a bark of laughter. "FBI, huh? That's cute. You expect us to believe that?"

"Doesn't matter if you believe me or not," Sofia replied, her tone clipped. "I'm warning you to stay away from me."

"Or what?" the tall one taunted, his voice dripping with disdain. "You'll arrest us?"

The trio closed in on her, their expressions a twisted mix of amusement and menace. Sofia's instincts screamed at her to run, but she knew that fleeing would only make them pursue her. She had to stand her ground.

"Back off," she warned again, her eyes darting between the three as they continued their advance. "You don't want to do this."

"Ooh, we're really scared now," the scar-faced man mocked, grinning wickedly. "Don't worry, sweetheart. We just want to have a little fun, that's all. It won't hurt...much."

The bearded man lunged at Sofia, his hand reaching out to grab her. In the split second before he made contact, she swung her leg up, connecting it with his wrist. The force of the kick sent him stumbling backward, a cry of pain escaping his lips.

"Damn," he hissed, cradling his injured arm. "You're tougher than you look."

"Leave me alone," Sofia said, her heart hammering in her chest. She knew she couldn't keep this up for long, but she refused to let fear take control.

"Hey, no hard feelings, right?" said the tall one, grinning as he approached her. "Just a little game, remember?"

Sofia's muscles tensed, ready to strike. As he lunged at her, she sidestepped and threw an elbow into his side. It connected with a dull thud, and he too stumbled back, gasping for breath. But despite their surprise, the men were far from defeated.

"Alright, enough playing around," growled the scar-faced man, his eyes narrowing as he studied Sofia. "We're not letting you get away that easily."

The three men exchanged glances, a silent understanding passing between them. They moved in unison, advancing on Sofia from different angles like a pack of wolves cornering their prey. She could

116

feel the icy tendrils of fear creeping up her spine, but she refused to give in to panic. Instead, she focused on the moment, on the adrenaline coursing through her veins and the steady rhythm of her heartbeat.

"Come on, sweetheart," taunted the bearded man, his voice dripping with contempt. "Let's see what else you've got."

As they charged toward her, Sofia realized she was outnumbered and outmatched. She couldn't fight all three at once; it was a losing battle. Her instincts screamed at her to run, to escape while she still had the chance.

In an instant, she spun on her heel and sprinted down the alley, her feet pounding against the cold pavement. The sound of the men's angry shouts filled the air, but she didn't look back. She couldn't afford to lose focus. All that mattered was putting as much distance between herself and her pursuers as possible.

Her muscles burned with the effort of outrunning her attackers, her lungs hungrily gulping down the cool night air. As she reached the street at the end of the alley, she dared a glance over her shoulder. To her relief, the three men had fallen behind, their faces twisted in frustration as they struggled to keep up. A triumphant grin tugged at the corner of Sofia's mouth, but it was short-lived.

The sudden screech of tires shattered the relative silence, and she barely had time to register the black sedan hurtling toward her before it made contact, knocking her off her feet. Pain exploded through her body as she hit the ground, the wind knocked out of her.

She lay there for a few moments, dazed. How badly had she been hurt? She tried to check in with her body, but all she felt was a dull ache in her hip. It seemed she'd been very fortunate.

The only problem was...why did it seem as if the sedan had swerved *toward* her at the last moment? If it had continued straight, it wouldn't have hit her.

Gritting her teeth, she pushed herself up to her knees, her limbs protesting the movement.

The driver's door creaked open, then slammed shut. Footsteps approached, heavy and deliberate.

Sofia glanced toward him, expecting to see someone concerned about her well-being (and, more than likely, afraid of a lawsuit). But the man bearing down on her had no such look. His eyes were cold, his body taut and rigid, like a coil ready to spring.

Panic flared within Sofia like a wildfire, threatening to overtake her thoughts. She needed to get up, needed to run, needed to get away before he reached her.

She pushed herself to her feet, her body aching with the effort. Just as she finished straightening, however, the man's fist flew toward her, blotting out the light.

And then Sofia felt her mind slipping away.

CHAPTER TWENTY FIVE

Santo's eyes darted rapidly from side to side, scanning the cobblestone street for any signs of onlookers. The dim glow of the streetlights flickered across the colorful papel picado banners that crisscrossed overhead, casting eerie shadows on the deserted sidewalks below.

It was past midnight in La Porta, California, and the Día de los Muertos celebration had wound down to a quiet murmur. A few stragglers could be seen in the distance, too absorbed in their own affairs to notice Santo's activities.

The purr of Santo's idling refrigeration truck filled the air as its headlights bathed the unconscious woman in a harsh white light. He studied her cautiously, his heart pounding with a mix of adrenaline and anxiety.

Crouching down beside her, Santo gently placed two fingers on her neck, feeling the steady throb of her pulse beneath his fingertips. She was dressed in a white lace dress, a shawl draped gracefully over her shoulders, her feet adorned with simple sandals. As Santo began to take in her appearance, his attention was drawn to a small object tucked discreetly at her waist. With a growing sense of unease, he retrieved it and found himself staring at an FBI badge.

"Shit," he muttered under his breath.

It must have been a trap, he thought, his fear mounting. *I knew it was too easy. She was luring me out into the open. She was the bait, and I snatched her up greedily.*

But if that was the case...where was the rest of her team? Surely they would close in now in order to protect her. They couldn't risk him harming her.

He scanned the desolate street, searching for any sign of lurking agents waiting to strike. But all he could see were the cobblestones glistening under the glow of the moonlight and the eerie shadows cast by the buildings that lined the street.

He exhaled slowly, the tension leaving his body in waves. Maybe she had been acting alone. If so, he could hardly believe his luck.

As if summoned by his thoughts, three men emerged from a nearby alley. They approached with purpose, their faces obscured by the darkness. For a split second, Santo thought they might indeed be federal agents descending on him.

But then he remembered who they were.

The first was tall and lanky, his movements like a feral cat stalking its prey. The second wore a tattered leather jacket and a sinister grin, revealing a row of crooked teeth gleaming in the dim light. The third man, shorter and stockier than the others, carried an air of menace, his eyes cold and calculating.

"Here," Santo said, reaching into his pocket and pulling out a wad of cash. He tossed it toward them, and the men scrambled to catch the fluttering bills. "Just as we agreed."

"Nice work," said the tall one, grinning as he divided the cash among them.

"Couldn't have done it without you," Santo replied, forcing a smile, though he couldn't shake the feeling that he'd made a deal with the devil. He hadn't needed them before, when he still had the element of surprise, but between the increased police presence and the warnings they'd sent out about his activities—well, he wasn't too proud to ask for a little help now and then.

One of the men, the tallest one with rough-looking stubble and a scar above his left eyebrow, tilted his head and stared at Santo, a predatory gleam in his eyes. "What are you going to do with her then?" he asked, nodding toward the unconscious woman.

"You don't need to know," Santo said, attempting to project confidence despite the chill creeping down his spine. "You did your part and got paid. That was the deal."

"Seems like such a waste for you to have her all to yourself," the man in the leather jacket sneered, stepping closer. The other two flanked him, their faces twisted into menacing grins, revealing yellowed teeth. Their dark eyes seemed void of anything remotely human, as if they had long ago surrendered any semblance of morality.

Adrenaline surged through Santo's veins as he realized they might beat him up and take the woman from him. He knew that if they sensed his fear, it would only fuel their aggressive intentions. He needed to regain control of the situation, and quickly.

Without a word, he calmly reached into his pocket and drew out a tecpatl, an ancient Aztec ceremonial knife, its obsidian blade shimmering ominously under the dim streetlight.

"Nice toy," one of the men scoffed, unimpressed.

"Ah, but this is no ordinary knife," Santo replied, his voice steady and cold. "This was once used for human sacrifices by Aztec priests.

The blade is coated with a poison so potent that even the slightest cut will prove fatal."

The shorter man snorted, clearly skeptical. "You're lying."

"Am I?" Santo asked, locking eyes with the disbeliever. "Why don't you come and try to take the woman from me? Then you'll see whether there's poison on the blade or not."

The trio of men eyed Santo with a mixture of unease and suspicion, the once-confident sneers on their faces replaced by a hesitant wariness. The streetlights cast elongated shadows that seemed to dance around them as they weighed his words.

"Let's go, boys," the tall one finally said, his voice laced with annoyance and frustration. "This one doesn't want to share."

With that, the three men retreated into the darkness of the alley from which they had emerged, leaving Santo alone with the unconscious woman.

Santo exhaled heavily, his breath visible in the cool night air as his heart raced with relief. He slid the tecpatl back into its hiding place within his jacket, grateful that his bluff had worked. There was no poison, but the fear it instilled had been enough to save him from a dangerous confrontation.

As he turned his attention back to the woman, he studied her delicate features, which were framed by her dark hair. She seemed almost angelic in her white lace dress, which made his purpose for her even more fitting.

Santo shook off any lingering hesitation and bent down, grabbing her beneath the armpits before dragging her toward the idling truck nearby.

Opening the back doors of the refrigeration truck, Santo faced the challenge of lifting the woman's limp form into the refrigerated compartment. Gritting his teeth, he hoisted her up onto his shoulder, the cold metal of the truck's exterior sending a shiver down his spine. With a grunt, he managed to maneuver her body into the chilly space, laying her down carefully among the crates and boxes filled with perishable goods.

The refrigerated compartment of the truck enveloped Santo and the woman in an icy embrace, the cold air stealing the warmth from their bodies. Santo's breath came out in frosty puffs, his heart pounding with adrenaline and a sense of urgency. The woman, still unconscious, stirred slightly, her moans barely audible. Her body shifted on the cold metal floor of the truck, the white lace of her dress contrasting sharply against the darkness that surrounded them.

Santo sprang into action, knowing he had little time to waste. He snatched a rough rope from the corner of the truck's interior, its frayed ends testament to previous uses. With swift, practiced movements, he bound the woman's wrists and ankles, ensuring she would not be able to escape if she were to awaken. His pulse raced, his hands trembling ever so slightly as he worked, aware of the high stakes involved.

Next, he retrieved a piece of cloth that lay crumpled by his feet. He slipped it around the woman's mouth, tying it securely at the back of her head. The makeshift gag would prevent any screams from alerting passersby to her plight.

"Just in case you decide to get chatty," he murmured.

As he stepped out of the refrigerated compartment and closed the doors behind him, he allowed himself a brief moment to reflect on the sacrifices he'd already made, the lives he'd taken in pursuit of lifting the ancient curse that haunted him. There was no turning back now. The end was in sight, and he could not afford to falter.

Santo climbed into the driver's seat, his hands gripping the steering wheel tightly. As the truck began to rumble along the cobblestone street, Santo's thoughts wandered to the woman he'd just kidnapped. She held the key to his salvation, to finally breaking free from the curse that had tormented him for so long. He knew what he had to do, and the terrible deed loomed before him like a specter.

"May the gods have mercy on us both," Santo murmured, his voice barely audible above the hum of the engine as he drove off into the night, the shadows swallowing them whole.

CHAPTER TWENTY SIX

Sofia's eyes flickered open, her vision blurred and shrouded in darkness. The bitter, biting cold seeped into her bones, and she shivered involuntarily.

Where am I? she wondered.

As she tried to move, she discovered her hands and ankles were bound together, the coarse ropes biting into her skin. To make matters worse, there was a rough cloth wrapped tightly around her mouth, stifling any cries for help.

What happened? she thought, her mind still foggy. Panic started to claw at the edges of her consciousness, but she forced herself to remain calm, drawing on her years of training as a special agent.

Gritting her teeth against the pain, she pushed herself up into a sitting position. Her head spun like a whirlwind, each movement sending waves of nausea through her body. It didn't take long for her to realize that someone had hit her hard in the head; the throbbing pain at the back of her skull seemed to echo throughout her entire being.

Stay focused, Sofia, she told herself, her thoughts a mixture of determination and fear. *You've been in worse situations before.*

In the suffocating darkness, she strained her ears to catch any hint of sound beyond her bleak confines. But there was nothing—only the distant, oppressive hum of silence. She knew she had found the killer she and Ryan were after, but now she was his captive, and it seemed as if Ryan and the rest of the world had vanished. Her heartbeat quickened at the thought that she might be his next victim.

She was not going down without a fight, though.

Gritting her teeth, she attempted to wriggle free from the tight ropes binding her hands and ankles. The coarse fibers dug into her skin, causing her to wince with pain. But no matter how hard she tried, she couldn't seem to loosen them. Panic clawed at her chest, threatening to consume her.

Relax...breathe, she commanded herself, forcing her breathing to slow. Succumbing to fear would only hinder her chances of escape. She needed to keep a clear head and think.

With her pulse steadying, Sofia assessed her situation. It felt like the temperature had dropped several degrees since she had regained consciousness. She knew that staying in this cold, dark place for too long could be fatal. Time was not on her side.

Focus on what you can control, she told herself, recalling advice from her years of training. If she couldn't untie the ropes, perhaps there was something else she could use to her advantage. She began to explore her surroundings.

Her fingers brushed against the cold floor beneath her, searching for anything that might aid in her escape. She could sense the moisture in the air, smell the faint aroma of mildew and gasoline. As she continued her search, she found herself growing more and more desperate. There had to be something, anything.

Come on, she thought, her frustration mounting. *You're a linguist, Sofia. You've deciphered ancient texts, unraveled mysteries that have baffled scholars for centuries. This is just another riddle for you to figure out.*

As her breathing slowed, her mind raced back to a memory from her time in Egypt. She had been working on deciphering ancient texts for a team of archaeologists when she met Rashid, a renowned escape artist who performed death-defying feats throughout the Middle East. Intrigued by his mysterious aura and captivating skill, Sofia had spent several nights observing him practice, hoping to learn something unique that might be useful one day.

"Remember, Sofia," Rashid had said in one of their rare moments alone, "the secret to escaping any bind is not brute force, but patience and focus." He demonstrated the technique, effortlessly slipping free from a tangle of ropes that moments before had seemed impenetrable.

Summoning the memory of Rashid's fluid movements, Sofia allowed herself to become hyper-aware of her body. She inhaled, feeling the air rush into her lungs, and then exhaled, letting all the tension leave her body. With relaxed arms, she gently twisted and maneuvered her hands.

Patience and focus, she repeated to herself. *Just stay relaxed.*

Minutes stretched out like hours as Sofia continued the delicate dance between breath and movement, her fingers growing numb from the effort. Centimeter by centimeter, the ropes began to move. Then, with one last deep inhale, she felt the ropes fall away, freeing her hands.

She quickly untied her ankles and removed the gag from her mouth. "Thank you, Rashid," she whispered.

Now liberated from her restraints, she cautiously crept through the dark interior, feeling the cold metal walls as she went. The scent of diesel fumes confirmed her suspicions: she was trapped in the back of a truck.

"Think, Sofia, think," she muttered to herself, her fingertips brushing over the cold metal doors that stood between her and freedom. Her fingers searched for a latch or an emergency release, but it became increasingly clear that the doors were locked from the outside.

"Damn it," she hissed, frustration building inside her. She had come so far, only to be stopped by a simple lock.

Her heart pounded in her chest as she paced back and forth, the cold metal floor sending shivers up her spine. She clenched and unclenched her fists, trying to think of a way out of this dark prison. But it felt as if her thoughts were stuck in a loop, unable to find a path forward.

"Damn it," she whispered under her breath, frustration boiling over. "There has to be some way out of here."

The darkness seemed to press in on her from all sides, suffocating her mind and stifling her creativity. And beneath the surface, a nagging fear gnawed at her, a constant reminder that she was trapped in the clutches of a killer. She knew that if she didn't escape soon, she might never get another chance.

"Focus, Sofia," she told herself, taking deep breaths to steady her nerves. "You've been through worse. You can do this."

But as the minutes ticked by, the situation began to feel increasingly hopeless. She fought back the urge to scream, to unleash her pent-up terror and frustration, knowing that it would only serve to alert her captor.

And then, just when despair threatened to overwhelm her, she heard it: the faint crunch of footsteps approaching from outside the truck. Her heart leaped into her throat, adrenaline flooding her system. This was it—her one chance to turn the tables on her captor.

Alright, you bastard, she thought, palms slick with sweat as she pressed herself against the cold metal wall beside the doors. *Let's see how* you *like being taken by surprise.*

CHAPTER TWENTY SEVEN

Sofia's heart pounded in her ears as the doors at the back of the cold compartment truck cracked open. A sliver of moonlight pierced through the darkness, illuminating the man's silhouette as he stood there, unsuspecting.

In one swift motion, Sofia sprang out of the truck, crashing into the man and tackling him to the ground. She landed hard and felt the air rush out of her lungs, but the adrenaline coursing through her veins kept her focused.

She rolled off the man and rose to a crouch, her eyes scanning the surroundings. They were in a parking lot behind a butcher's shop, the faint scent of blood and raw meat lingering in the air. An eerie silence enveloped the area, broken only by the distant echo of footsteps on the pavement. The glow from the streetlights cast an ominous yellow haze over the scene, revealing the darkened windows of the butcher's shop where slabs of meat hung on hooks inside like macabre ornaments.

She suspected she was still in La Porta, but beyond that she had no idea where she was. And right now, she didn't need to know.

The man's eyes, a shade of obsidian that seemed to swallow the surrounding light, locked onto Sofia as he rose unsteadily to his feet. He stood at an imposing height, towering over her, with broad shoulders and sinewy muscles that rippled beneath his tattered clothing. A jagged scar marred the side of his face, giving him a sinister appearance that sent shivers down Sofia's spine.

"Who are you?" she demanded, narrowing her eyes as she studied the stranger in front of her.

"Tu peor pesadilla," he replied, his voice a guttural growl that seemed to reverberate through the air. "Your worst nightmare."

As he spoke, the man drew a knife from the folds of his clothing. It was not just any knife, however, but a tecpatl, an Aztec ceremonial weapon with a curved blade fashioned from intricately carved obsidian. The hilt, adorned with feathers and beads, contrasted sharply with the lethal gleam of the blade, which caught the dim light of the streetlamp and reflected it back in a menacing dance of shadows.

Sofia's heart hammered against her ribcage as the man lunged forward, brandishing the knife with practiced ease. She dodged to the side, narrowly avoiding the deadly arc of the blade, and backed up toward the butcher's shop. Her breath came in short gasps, the adrenaline coursing through her veins and fueling her every move.

He snarled, slashing at her again. This time, Sofia was prepared. As the blade came hurtling toward her, she kicked out, striking his wrist with her shin. The impact was bone-jarring. The knife flew from the man's hand, clattering to the ground several feet away.

For a moment the man just stood there, wincing as he cradled his wrist. Then he glanced up. His expression was fierce and furious, full of unchecked rage.

"You don't have to make this any worse—" Sofia was saying, but the man cut her off with a primal scream. He charged at her like a mad bull, his eyes wild with fury. Before she could react, he slammed into her, the impact driving them both backward until they crashed against the door behind her.

With a creaking groan, the old wooden door gave way beneath their combined weight and swung open. Sofia felt a sickening sensation of weightlessness as they tumbled through the dark void beyond the doorway, careening down a flight of stairs.

She flailed helplessly, grasping for something – anything – to halt her descent, but there was nothing to hold onto. The stairs seemed to go on forever, each one slamming into her body with bruising force. Her vision blurred, the world around her reduced to a disorienting swirl of darkness and pain.

Finally, mercifully, the fall came to an end. Sofia landed hard on the cold, unforgiving concrete floor of the cellar, the breath knocked from her lungs. She lay there for a moment, dazed and disoriented, trying to make sense of what had just happened. Her head throbbed, and she could feel the warm trickle of blood dripping from a gash on her forehead.

As her eyes slowly adjusted to the dim light, she realized that she was surrounded by row upon row of slabs of meat hanging on hooks, their surfaces slick and glistening in the faint glow of a single naked bulb overhead. The air was frigid, biting at her exposed skin and sending involuntary shivers through her battered body.

A few feet away, the man lay sprawled on the ground, groaning in pain. Despite the agony coursing through her own body, Sofia couldn't help but feel a grim sense of satisfaction at the sight.

Her heart hammered in her chest as she locked eyes with her attacker. He was getting back on his feet, and so was she. In the dim light of the cold, dank cellar, she noticed a table nearby, laden with an array of butcher tools: knives, cleavers, hooks, and similar items.

They both lunged for it at the same time, their desperation fueling their movements. But the man was closer, and reached it first. His hand closed around the handle of a large, wicked-looking cleaver.

Sofia backed away from him, her breath coming in ragged gasps, her pulse pounding in her ears.

The man darted toward her, slashing with the cleaver. Sofia dodged to the side, narrowly avoiding the lethal blade. The chilling sensation of cold metal grazing her arm sent shivers down her spine.

She stumbled backward and bumped into one of the slabs of meat hanging behind her. Desperate to stay out of reach, she continued to retreat, feeling the blood from the carcasses seeping into her clothes, making them stick to her skin.

"Where are you going?" the man taunted, advancing on her with a twisted grin. "There's nowhere left to run."

As he swung the cleaver at her again, Sofia's instincts kicked in and she grabbed one of the hanging slabs of meat, swinging it in front of her just in time.

The cleaver sank deep into the meat, lodging itself in the bone. The man grasped it with both hands, trying to pull the blade free, but it was stuck fast.

Sofia saw her chance and took it. With all the strength she could muster, she kicked him hard in the stomach, causing him to double over in pain.

She advanced on the man, her dark eyes focused and unyielding. With a swift kick to his chest, she forced him back, gaining the upper hand for the first time since their deadly dance had begun.

As she continued to drive him back, the man's once-confident expression began to falter, replaced by a mixture of fear and rage. He was losing control, and he knew it. She could see the panic rising in his eyes, and it only fueled her determination.

"We're going to finish this now," she said, her voice low and dangerous. "I won't let you hurt anyone else."

As she closed the distance with the man, however, her foot slipped in a puddle of blood on the cold, wet floor. She lost her balance and fell hard, the air knocked from her lungs in a violent gasp.

She heard a rush of footsteps as the man raced toward her. She braced herself, expecting him either to pick up the cleaver again or else try to strangle her with his hands, but instead she heard the whoosh of a door opening. A gust of air even chillier than the temperature already in the room drew gooseflesh across her body.

Just as she started to rise, the man grabbed a handful of her hair and began dragging her across the floor. She screamed, desperately trying to get to her feet, but her limbs betrayed her, refusing to cooperate in her moment of need.

The man's grip on her hair tightened, his breath hot and rancid against her ear as he forced her into a small freezer compartment.

"Adiós, bonita," he sneered, his voice dripping with malice. And before Sofia could muster the strength to fight him off, the door slammed shut in her face, plunging her into darkness once more.

CHAPTER TWENTY EIGHT

Sofia's breath formed a foggy cloud in front of her face as she desperately tried to open the walk-in freezer door. It refused to budge, however; just like the doors on the truck, it was designed to only be opened from the outside.

The frigid air bit through her thin clothes, and the cold crept under her skin, chilling her to the bone. She shivered uncontrollably, and her teeth chattered in the bitter cold.

No, no, no, she thought.

She took a moment to study her surroundings. The dimly lit freezer was filled with packaged frozen meat hanging on hooks, their surfaces glistening with frost in the weak light. Sofia could make out the carcasses of pigs and cows, their eyes staring blankly at her. In another corner lay stacks of neatly wrapped cuts, labeled and ready for delivery. The grisly scene only added to her mounting dread.

"Help!" She banged on the door, her voice cracking with desperation. "Is anyone there? Please!"

A sinister laugh echoed through the metal walls, sending shivers down Sofia's spine. "You can scream all you want, but nobody will hear you," the man said from the other side of the door. His voice sounded muffled, yet the cruelty in his voice was crystal clear.

"What do you want?" Sofia asked, trying to collect her thoughts even as her body succumbed to the relentless cold.

"Nothing that you can give me," he replied ominously. "I already have what I want."

Sofia's mind raced, attempting to decipher the meaning behind his cryptic words. But as the cold continued to seep into her bones and her hope of escape dwindled, she knew she had to act quickly if she wanted to survive this nightmare.

"This is madness!" she cried. "You're insane, you know that?"

"Actually I'm quite sane." The man's voice became more animated, as if he were about to share an age-old secret. "There is an ancient Aztec curse, you see, that has plagued my family for generations. And I have finally discovered a way to get rid of it."

"Indeed," he continued, his tone almost reverential. "My ancestors angered the gods with their hubris, and we have been cursed ever since.

The only way to lift this curse is through human sacrifice, a ritual that must be performed with precision and care."

"And...what? I'm supposed to be one of your sacrifices?"

"Your fate was sealed long before we crossed paths," he replied cryptically. "It's not personal, merely a necessity. The curse takes many forms: disease, misfortune, even death. For my family to finally live free of its grip, I must complete the ritual."

Sofia tried to think of something to say, some way to persuade him to abandon this mad path. But how was she supposed to change his mind when he was so set on a course of action?

"How do you know this curse is real?" she asked. "How has your family suffered?"

"Oh, we have suffered in ways you cannot even imagine," he said, his voice full of bitterness. "My great-grandfather lost his entire fortune to a fire that destroyed his factory. My grandfather died of a mysterious illness, and my father took his own life after the curse drove him to insanity. It is only through researching our family history that I have discovered the true cause of our misfortunes."

"Listen," Sofia said, her voice steady despite the fear that gripped her. "There has to be another way. Killing me won't lift any curse. It's just an excuse for you to act out your violent fantasies. Why don't we talk about this? Maybe there's a way we can help you find a different solution."

She waited, holding her breath. In the silence that followed, she heard a voice, but it was not the man's voice. This voice was softer, feminine.

"Oh, don't worry about that," the man said, apparently addressing the other speaker. "Your part in this will be over soon enough."

A cold realization gripped Sofia's heart: The killer already had his next victim. If she didn't find a way to get out and stop him, another innocent life would be lost.

"Wait!" she shouted, her voice cracking from the cold. "The curse you spoke of...it only demands four human sacrifices, right?"

The answer was slow, surprised. "Yes. How did you know that?"

Sofia ignored the question. "You've already taken three lives. That leaves just one left to fulfill the ritual. Let the other woman go, and take me instead."

There was a pause, and then the man laughed, the sound chilling her to the bone. "As noble as your offer is, Special Agent Blake," he said, his voice dripping with contempt, "you've actually miscounted. The first woman I killed was merely practice—she didn't count toward

131

the total for the sacrifice. I needed to prepare myself for the work that was to come."

Sofia's heart sank as the pieces fell into place. Now she understood why the first victim had been killed before the festival started, and why they hadn't discovered a calavera on the first victim as they had with the others. It had all been a twisted rehearsal for the horror that was unfolding now.

"Make no mistake, agent," the man said. "Both you and this woman shall be sacrificed, completing the ritual and stopping the curse. You ought to feel honored for being chosen to take part in such a sacred rite. If you really understood just how momentous, how significant this moment is..."

His muffled words went on, but Sofia had stopped listening. She was focused solely on finding a way out of her icy tomb. There had to be some means of escape, some weakness she could exploit.

The frigid air bit at her skin as she searched the interior of the freezer, her hands trembling from both the cold and the adrenaline pumping through her veins. Her breaths came in shallow gasps, forming small clouds of vapor that quickly dissipated into the darkness.

As she moved along the walls, her fingers traced over the seams and edges of the metal panels, searching for any sign of a vent or loose fixture. Her heart raced with each passing moment, each second bringing her closer to the inevitable.

Finally, her numb fingers brushed against an irregularity in the surface, and she felt a surge of hope. There, midway along the wall, was a small vent, its grate obscured by frost. An HVAC vent, she guessed. A faint glimmer of light seeped through the slits, beckoning to her like a beacon in the night.

Determined not to let this opportunity slip away, Sofia braced herself against the wall and kicked at the vent with all the strength she could muster. The metal groaned in protest, but eventually yielded under the force of her assault, the grate clattering to the floor.

Without wasting another moment, Sofia hoisted herself up into the narrow opening.

Whoever that other woman was, Sofia was her only hope—and she refused to let her down.

CHAPTER TWENTY NINE

Sofia winced as the sharp edges of the vent dug into her flesh. The passage was tight and claustrophobic, and so cold that she felt her whole body shuddering. Numbness spread through her hands, across her face.

The muffled sound of the man's chanting reached her ears as if from a world away, his voice rising and falling in a sinister cadence. The realization that she was the only person who could stop that man from his devilish plans injected her with a fresh sense of resolve, and she forced herself forward.

Reaching a second grate, she searched for a latch or some other way to open it, but there was nothing. Panic crept up on her as the chilly air continued to wash over her, cramping her muscles.

Unsure what else to do, she turned around in the vent, her limbs folding painfully against her body as she navigated the narrow space. Then, with her feet in front of her, she kicked at the vent. Each blow sent a jarring pain up her body.

On the fourth or fifth kick, the cover fell off. She crawled forward and dropped hard on the concrete floor, too numb and desperate to slow her fall. For a few moments she lay there, her body shaking, her teeth chattering, and her hands unfeeling.

Come on, Sofia, she told herself. *Don't give up now.*

Glancing to the side, she saw something that caused her blood to run even colder, if that were possible. In the center of the room, amid slabs of meat hanging from hooks, a woman was suspended upside down, unconscious and bound by ropes tied tightly around her ankles. The ropes looped around a meat hook embedded in the ceiling, leaving her body to dangle mere feet above the ground. Beneath her a metal bowl rested on the floor, poised – presumably – to catch the blood that would spill from her throat.

Beside the woman stood the man, his face contorted into an expression of twisted fervor. His voice rose and fell in a rhythmic chant as he clutched a tecpatl – an obsidian knife – in one hand and a calavera in the other. The sound of his voice rebounded off the walls, adding to the oppressive atmosphere of the room.

A chill ran down her spine as the reality of the situation took hold, and she knew she had to act quickly. Her body, however, was still recovering from the cold of the freezer, and though she was steadily thawing in the relatively warm air outside the freezer, it still took all her strength just to rise from the floor.

"Stop!" she shouted, her voice slicing through the sinister chanting like a razor. The man's head snapped toward her, his eyes narrowing with surprise and annoyance.

"You're a stubborn one, aren't you? I suppose I shouldn't have expected that freezer to hold you for long. No matter—you will simply have to wait your turn. It won't be long now."

Sofia fought to keep her fear in check, knowing she couldn't afford to show weakness. She had faced dangerous criminals before, but this man was different. His beliefs and motivations made him unpredictable and terrifying.

She watched as he prepared to cut the woman's throat, positioning the razor-sharp obsidian blade against her delicate skin. Panic welled up within Sofia, and she knew she had to do something – anything – to save the woman's life.

Just then the woman's eyes fluttered open, her pupils dilating in the dim light as she registered her predicament. A muffled scream tore through the gag in her mouth, her body writhing and twisting in a futile attempt to free herself from the ropes that bound her.

Sofia's heart clenched at the sight, her mind racing with a thousand different strategies to save the woman while buying more time for herself. The man, still leering at Sofia, noticed the woman's awakening and promptly set the calavera down on a nearby table.

"Ah, you're finally awake," he cooed, his voice dripping with false sweetness. He reached out and gently caressed the woman's face, as if trying to soothe her terror. "Don't worry, my dear. It will all be over soon." His fingers traced her cheek before wrapping around her chin, forcing her to look into his cold, merciless eyes.

"Please," Sofia whispered, her voice cracking as she fought to keep her composure. She needed to distract him, to give the woman a chance to escape, to find a way to end this nightmare without further bloodshed. "There must be another way."

The man's grip tightened on the woman's chin, his other hand raising the tecpatl to her throat. "This is the only way," he insisted, his gaze never leaving the woman's. "Her sacrifice is the only way to break the curse."

Sofia's thoughts raced, searching for some leverage against the man's unwavering conviction. Every moment she felt her body warming, becoming more responsive and stronger. But if she tried to act now, she would probably only cause the woman to die faster. So what could she do?

"I wouldn't do that if I were you," she said. "There's a team of federal agents closing in on us as we speak, so you'll just be incriminating yourself further. You won't get the chance to finish the ritual—and thus, you won't be able to lift the curse."

The man laughed, the sound resonating through the dimly lit warehouse like a sinister melody. "You lie," he declared, his voice dripping with disdain. "If there were others, they would have stormed this place already. You're alone, and you know it."

As he spoke, Sofia's keen eyes flicked to the captive woman. She observed the frantic movements of her fingers, inching closer to loosening the ropes that bound her.

I need to buy her time, Sofia thought. *Maybe if I can do that, she can get a hand free.*

"Perhaps I *am* alone," she conceded, her voice steady despite the pounding of her heart. "But don't underestimate my knowledge. I understand the meaning of the skulls and the curse. The ancient Aztecs are a fascinating civilization, don't you agree?"

The man's gaze shifted from the woman back to Sofia, curiosity gleaming in his eyes. "So you comprehend the significance of what I'm about to do?" he asked, tilting his head slightly. "Why, then, do you seek to stop me? Don't you grasp the importance of lifting this curse?"

Sofia allowed herself a small smile, feeling the power balance shift ever so slightly in her favor. She had piqued his interest, and now it was crucial to keep him engaged while the captive woman continued her struggle.

Sofia's eyes darted between the man and the woman, noticing the delicate movement of the latter's fingers as she worked to free her hand. Every second was crucial, and Sofia needed to maintain the captor's attention just a bit longer.

"Actually," she began, feigning nonchalance while inching closer, "I've come to realize that the curse you believe in...it isn't real."

The temperature in the room seemed to drop several degrees. The man's expression transformed from curiosity to icy fury. His grip on the tecpatl tightened.

"You dare?" he hissed, his voice barely more than a whisper. "You presume to know better than the ancients? The curse is very real, I assure you. And now, you've just sealed your fate along with hers."

Sofia's heart hammered against her ribcage. She had miscalculated, and she knew it. But there was no turning back now. She searched for any hint of doubt in the man's eyes, grasping for another opportunity to stall him. Yet, all she could see was unwavering conviction.

As the man's gaze returned to the terrified woman, Sofia's thoughts raced alongside the adrenaline pumping through her veins. This was it—her moment of truth. She had to act now or risk losing everything.

"Think about it," she said urgently, knowing her words were likely futile but unwilling to give up. "If the curse is real, then why hasn't it been lifted before now? Surely others have tried."

He didn't even grace her with a glance this time. Instead, his focus was entirely on the woman's throat, the blade poised just above her skin.

In a desperate attempt to buy more time, Sofia drew upon her expertise in linguistics. She recited the ancient curse in perfect Nahuatl, the words rolling off her tongue like a sacred chant. *"Miquiztli ya tlayohua, teēyōtl īpan tōnalmachiyōtia. Tēpanīlli tonatiuh, yancuīc tlācatiyān."*

The man froze, his eyes widening in shock as he slowly turned to face her. His grip on the tecpatl wavered, and for a brief moment, his iron resolve seemed to falter. "You...you speak Nahuatl?" he stammered, disbelief etched across his face.

Sofia held her breath, hoping that her gamble would pay off. She could see the woman's fingers working furiously at her bonds, desperately trying to free her hand. "I've studied many languages and cultures," she said, her voice steady despite her racing heart. "Nahuatl is just one of them."

His eyes narrowed suspiciously, but the surprise in his expression remained. "That doesn't change anything," he hissed, turning back toward the woman. The blade of the tecpatl gleamed ominously in the dim light as he raised it to her throat. "This curse must be lifted!"

Sofia's pulse quickened, adrenaline surging through her veins as she lunged forward. Time seemed to slow, each second stretching into an eternity as she raced toward the man. But even as her muscles strained with the effort, she knew she wouldn't reach him in time.

Just as the sharp edge of the tecpatl was about to pierce the woman's vulnerable flesh, however, her hand broke free from its bindings. With a strength born of desperation, she grasped the man's wrist, halting the knife's deadly descent.

With a final burst of speed, Sofia closed the distance between them, launching herself at the man with all the force she could muster. The impact sent them crashing to the cold, concrete floor, and there was a meaty thud as the man's head bounced off the concrete, dazing him.

Gritting her teeth, Sofia wrenched the man's arm behind his back with a swift, decisive motion. The sharp sound of his gasp cut through the chill air as he dropped the knife, the clatter of metal against concrete sounding sharply inside the confines of the room.

"Get up," she said, hauling him to his feet by the twisted arm. She could feel the heat of his anger radiating off him like a furnace, but she knew she couldn't afford to let him regain control. Her mind raced, trying to come up with a plan while her body remained tense and coiled for action.

Her gaze flicked around the room, searching for something – anything – that might help her subdue the man, since she didn't have her handcuffs with her, having left them in the alley with her pile of clothes. The fluorescent lights above cast grotesque shadows on the slabs of meat hanging from hooks nearby, their pallid flesh marred by streaks of crimson.

And then her eyes fell upon the freezer door.

CHAPTER THIRTY

It's finally over, Sofia thought.

The first faint light of dawn cast a soft glow over La Porta as she watched several police officers escort a man in handcuffs up from the basement of the butcher shop where she herself had been held captive not long before. The man was large, with a barrel chest and thick forearms, his once neatly combed hair now disheveled and matted with sweat. A look of defeat clouded his sunken eyes, and he shivered violently—whether from fear or the lingering cold of the freezer where he'd been imprisoned, Sofia couldn't be sure.

Ryan chuckled softly beside her, the sound almost lost in the distant hum of early morning traffic. "I still can't believe you locked him in a freezer," he said, his eyes twinkling with amusement. "Now that's poetic justice."

"Believe me," Sofia replied, her dark hair falling over one shoulder as she turned to face her partner, "it wasn't my first choice. But he did the same thing to me, and I didn't have my handcuffs. I had to keep him confined somehow until the police arrived." Her voice was matter of fact, the words spoken by someone who had faced danger countless times and lived to tell the tale.

"I'm just glad he was too big to fit through that vent," she said. "Either that, or he didn't find it. I stood there waiting just in case he tried to crawl through, but all he did was bang on the door and hurl curses at me."

Ryan nodded, a smile playing at the corners of his mouth. "Well, it was certainly creative." His gaze shifted from the killer to Sofia, and his brow furrowed slightly. "But what's with the outfit? You look like you're going to a garden party, not hunting down a serial killer." He gestured at her white lace dress, the delicate fabric contrasting sharply with the grime and darkness that surrounded them.

Sofia glanced down at herself, taking in the shawl draped around her shoulders and the sandals on her feet. "It's a long story," she said with a sigh, feeling the weight of the night's events settling on her like a heavy cloak.

"We've got time."

She watched as the man disappeared into the back of a waiting police car. She thought of the three men attacking her in the alley, and of waking in the cold compartment truck, and of the time during which she had been trapped in the freezer. She'd felt so powerless in those moments, so vulnerable and alone. But now, with Ryan by her side and the killer in custody, she felt a sense of relief wash over her.

"I'll tell you another time," she said, not wishing to relive those moments just now. As she faced Ryan, he took a hissing breath.

"What happened to your face?" he asked, frowning with concern. "You've got a huge bruise on the side of your head."

"Must be where he kicked me." She touched the bruise with her fingertips, then winced at the pain.

Ryan clenched his jaw, his nostrils flaring. "Good thing the police got to him before I did. I'm not sure I would've been so gentle."

The wail of sirens faded into the distance as the first light of dawn began to edge over the horizon. As Sofia glanced around, taking in the aftermath of the night's events, the faint sound of footsteps caught her attention.

Turning toward the noise, she saw a woman approaching. Her heart quickened with recognition—this was the woman who had been hanging upside down in the basement, moments away from becoming another victim of the killer's depraved ritual. Now she walked with a shaky gait, her face pale and drawn but otherwise unharmed. The paramedics had apparently given her a once-over, wrapping her in a foil blanket to ward off the lingering chill.

"Thank you so much," the woman whispered, her voice trembling with emotion as she threw her arms around Sofia. "You saved my life."

"Hey, it's okay," Sofia murmured, returning the embrace, acutely aware of the woman's shivering form pressed against her own. They had come so close to death that the very fact they were both still alive was nothing short of a miracle.

The woman stepped back, her eyes glistening with unshed tears. "I'm sorry, I didn't mean to... I just wanted to say thank you." She took a deep breath, as if steeling herself, and extended a hand. "I'm Emily."

"Sofia," she replied, clasping Emily's hand firmly. "Special Agent Sofia Blake."

Emily's gaze turned to Ryan. "I don't know if you know this already, but this woman's incredible. I don't know what would have happened to me if she hadn't been there."

"She is," Ryan agreed, his eyes glinting with pride.

Sofia offered Emily a small, reassuring smile, even as her mind churned with thoughts of what could have been, the darkness that had nearly swallowed them both. But it hadn't. They were here, alive and breathing, and that was enough for now.

"I'm curious, Emily," she said. "How did you end up down there?"

"He followed me into a restroom," Emily murmured, her voice still shaky. "He knocked me out and when I woke up, I was...tied up like that." She shuddered at the memory.

Sofia placed a comforting hand on Emily's arm, feeling the warmth of her skin through the foil blanket.

"What about you?" Emily asked. "Did he dress you up like this, or were you undercover?"

"Undercover," Sofia said, aware that Ryan would be listening. "I was hoping it would work, and it did."

Emily stared at her in silence for a few seconds as the implication set in. "You dressed like that just to get his attention so he'd try to abduct you? You put yourself in danger like that just to find me?"

"Sometimes," Sofia said softly, "we have to take risks in order to save others. It was the only play I had."

"Thank you," Emily whispered again, her voice thick with gratitude. "I don't know what else to say." With tears streaking her face, she hugged Sofia once more before turning to leave, the blanket billowing around her like a protective cloak.

"Take care of yourself, Emily," Sofia called after her, watching as the woman was guided toward an ambulance by a pair of paramedics, presumably to run further tests at the hospital just to make doubly sure she was okay.

"Are you insane?" Ryan's voice cut through the silence that had settled around them. "You deliberately tried to lure the killer to yourself—without anyone watching your back, no less?"

Sofia turned to face her partner, his concern evident in the furrow of his brow and the tense set of his jaw. "I tried to reach you, but I couldn't. You were probably still questioning Besser."

"And what about the police? You couldn't tell them?"

"There was no time to make such a plan. I needed to act fast, and involving the police would have only increased the risk of tipping our hand."

Ryan took a deep breath and let it out slowly, shaking his head. "Come on," Sofia said softly, trying to get a smile out of him. "You're the one who fought Hector in that underground ring."

"It was our only choice."

"Are you trying to tell me you didn't enjoy it?"

There was a mischievous twinkle in his eye. "Well, of course I enjoyed it, but that was different. Besides, we can't *both* be reckless. I need you to balance me out, keep me from going over the edge."

Sofia smiled and placed a hand on his shoulder. "Next time I'm thinking of wandering the streets during Día de los Muertos to lure a serial killer out of hiding, I'll be sure to let you know—assuming you answer your phone, that is."

He grunted. "Fair enough."

Ryan's eyes darted away from Sofia, catching sight of a uniformed officer standing at the door to the butcher's shop, signaling him over. "I have to go talk to Officer Martinez," he said. "They're looking at the blood in the basement, making sure it's animal blood and not from other victims we don't know about."

Sofia nodded. "Do what you gotta do."

"You'll be okay? You won't try to lure in any other creeps while I'm gone?"

She laughed softly and pushed his shoulder. "Get out of here."

As Ryan disappeared into the throng, Ethan Knight approached, a steaming cup of Mexican hot chocolate cradled in his hands. The rich, spicy aroma wafted through the chilly air, and Sofia felt herself shivering involuntarily.

Ethan handed her the cup with a warm smile. "Thought you might need this after such an intense night," he said, shaking his head admiringly.

"Thanks, Ethan," she murmured, wrapping her cold fingers around the warmth of the cup. She took a small sip, savoring the rich flavor and feeling it spread through her like liquid courage. "You didn't have to do that."

"Actually, I did," he replied, his eyes holding hers. "You did great work tonight, Sofia, saving that woman's life."

"Thank you," she said, looking down at the swirling depths of her hot chocolate, her cheeks coloring slightly. "I just did what I had to do."

"No, no. Don't give me that 'it's all part of the job' BS. What you did was exceptionally brave—reckless, maybe, but brave."

Sofia smiled wryly, recalling Ryan's similar assessment. "Seems to be the general consensus around here."

Ethan chuckled, leaning against the wall beside her. "Well, they're not wrong. You put your own life on the line to save someone else's. That takes guts."

She looked up at him, her eyes meeting his. They held the moment for a second, and Sofia felt a tiny flutter in her chest before breaking his gaze and taking another sip of her hot chocolate.

"So," Ethan said, "what's next for you? Another case, another monster to collar?"

"After a shower, a good night's rest, and a hot meal, sure."

Ethan chuckled. They were both silent for several moments.

"Speaking of meals," Ethan said, "we should break bread together some time. Or have coffee—I'm down with either."

"I'd like that," Sofia said, somewhat surprised by the offer but feeling a spark of anticipation deep within her.

Ethan sighed dramatically. "It's too bad I don't have any way to reach you, isn't it?"

Smiling, Sofia said, "That depends on whether or not you have your phone on you."

Ethan frowned, fumbled around in his pocket for a moment, and then pulled out his phone, his eyes widening in mock surprise. "Well, look at that! I *do* have it."

Sofia gave him her number, and he put it into his phone.

"Give me a call sometime," she said with a playful shrug of her shoulder. She thought of mentioning that she had tried calling him earlier, but she decided not to. Better to play it cool. She didn't want him to think she was desperate, even if she'd had a professional reason for making the call.

He pushed off from the wall. "You know what? I think I just might. For now, though, I'll get out of your hair."

She smiled. "Take it easy, Ethan."

"You, too." He winked at her.

The heavy scent of disinfectant wafted through the air as Sofia watched Ethan's retreating form, feeling the weight of the past few hours bearing down upon her. Her dark hair was a tangled mess and her dress clung to her body, damp with perspiration and fear. She wrapped her arms around herself in an attempt to dispel the lingering chill from her time in the freezer.

"Hey, Sof," Ryan said as he rejoined her, his brow furrowed with concern. "What did Ethan want?"

"Nothing much," she said nonchalantly, trying to downplay the conversation. "Just checking up on me, I suppose."

"Ah, okay." He eyed her for a moment, taking note of the fatigue etched across her features. "You look exhausted. Let me drive you home so you can get some rest."

"Thanks, Ryan. I'd appreciate that." she agreed quietly, eager to escape the macabre scene unfolding before them.

As they made their way toward Ryan's truck, Sofia glanced back at the basement entrance of the butcher shop where she had nearly met her end. The darkness that seemed to emanate from the depths below sent an involuntary shudder down her spine, a stark reminder of how close she had come to failing to escape its chilly embrace.

"Are you sure you're alright?" Ryan asked, pulling her attention back to the present.

She shook her head slightly, as if trying to dislodge the memories that threatened to consume her. "I will be," she assured him, attempting a weak smile. "I just need some sleep."

He opened her door for her, and she slid into the seat and fastened her seatbelt. As the engine roared to life, she leaned her head against the cool glass of the window, gazing out as dawn broke across the world, chasing away the shadows, purifying the night.

Before the truck had gone a hundred feet, she was asleep.

EPILOGUE

Sofia waved, watching as Ryan's truck disappeared around the corner, leaving her standing alone on the sidewalk. The air was crisp and cool, a gentle breeze teasing loose strands of her dark hair. A shiver ran down her spine as she shifted the bundle of old clothes in her arm, her gun nestled securely within.

Exhaustion weighed heavily on her, her eyes bloodshot and stinging from the night's work. Her body longed for the comfort of a warm shower and the solace of sleep. She turned toward her house, its quaint charm apparent even in the dim light.

As Sofia approached, the neighborhood seemed to come alive with the soft chatter of birds and the distant hum of morning traffic. Each house had its own unique character, their well-manicured lawns, and blooming flowers a testament to the pride the residents took in their homes. But it was Sofia's historical house that held her heart captive.

Once a haven for artists and writers during the roaring twenties, her California abode still bore the elegant lines and craftsmanship of a bygone era. Intricate woodwork framed the wide windows, and a deep porch wrapped around the front, inviting visitors to sit and stay awhile. It was a house with a story, much like Sofia herself, and she couldn't help but feel a kinship with its walls.

She walked up the stone path, her footsteps echoing softly in the stillness. As she neared the door, she paused for a moment, allowing herself to drink in the sight of her beloved home. Her mind wandered to the countless secrets it held, the whispered conversations and stolen moments forever etched into its foundations. If only those walls could talk, she thought, what tales they would have to tell.

Sofia's fingers wrapped around the cold metal handle of the door, and as she stepped inside, her senses were immediately greeted by a myriad of memories. The walls of the hallway were adorned with intricately carved wooden masks from her time in Bali, their haunting eyes seeming to follow her every move. The scent of sandalwood incense drifted through the air, transporting her back to the bustling markets of Marrakech. A beautifully embroidered tapestry momentarily distracted her from her exhaustion, its vibrant colors taking her back to her time in India.

Upon reaching the kitchen, Sofia set the bundle of clothes and her gun on the countertop and poured herself a glass of water. The cool liquid provided a momentary relief, and her thoughts turned to her conversation with Ethan Knight. She thought of the casual, playful way he'd asked for her number.

"Maybe it wouldn't be so bad, having someone around," she mused, swirling the remaining water in her glass, the ice clinking against the sides. The truth was that she hadn't dated much in recent years; her work consumed most of her time, leaving little room for anything else. But there was something about Ethan – his intelligence, his passion for Mesoamerican languages – that intrigued her.

"Perhaps it's time I allowed myself some happiness," she murmured to the empty kitchen, the words lingering in the air like a long-forgotten promise. It wasn't just the thrill of having someone new in her life that tempted her, but also the possibility of sharing her world with another soul, someone who could understand her and appreciate the depth of her experiences.

With a sigh, Sofia set down her empty glass and gazed around her kitchen, taking in the eclectic array of souvenirs that reminded her of the life she had built for herself—a life that was equal parts adventure and loneliness. In the dim light of the early morning, it seemed as though her home was whispering to her, urging her to take a chance on something new, on someone who could bring a spark of excitement into her carefully guarded world.

And as she stood there, surrounded by the memories of her past and the potential of her future, Sofia felt a flicker of hope ignite within her heart. Perhaps, just perhaps, it was time for her to step out of the shadows and embrace the possibility of a shared life.

Her body did not allow her to dwell on this for long, however. Weariness weighed down on her like the dense fog hugging the California coast. She trudged up the stairs, her damp hair clinging to her neck like tendrils of seaweed. The shadows in her home seemed to be whispering secrets she could not quite decipher, beckoning her to surrender to the embrace of sleep.

She reached her bedroom, the door creaking open as if in protest of her intrusion. Her sanctuary was a harmonious blend of the old and the new. Dark wooden furniture, relics from another era, stood sentinel against the muted beige walls adorned with vibrant paintings and tapestries from her travels. In one corner, a carved mahogany dresser held court, its surface a veritable shrine to her late grandmother—a delicate lace doily, an antique silver brush, a faded photograph capturing a moment of laughter frozen in time.

"Another day," Sofia murmured, closing the curtains to shut out the creeping dawn. She glanced at her reflection in the full-length mirror, her eyes rimmed with shadows that told of a long, sleepless night. A wistful smile tugged at her lips, and she whispered, "Perhaps things will change soon."

With a sigh, she sank into her bed, the plush duvet enveloping her like a cloud. As she lay there, a thousand thoughts clamored for her attention, but she pushed them away, willing herself to find solace in the darkness.

"Enough," she muttered, turning onto her side. "I need to rest."

But even as she tried to escape into the realm of dreams, her gaze was drawn upwards, toward the ceiling that loomed above her like an ever-present reminder of the life she had chosen. Every inch of it was covered in a tangled web of case notes, strings, tacks, and photographs—a living canvas of the mystery she'd never been able to solve.

What happened to my sister? she wondered. *Where did she go, and where is she now?*

A single tear traced its way down Sofia's cheek. She looked up again, studying the notes of the cold case, grief gripping her heart like a vice.

Yes, it was time to get back to searching. Time to solve the one mystery that had eluded her for so many years.

NOW AVAILABLE!

NO ONE LEFT
(A Sofia Blake FBI Suspense Thriller —Book Two)

FBI special agent Sofia Blake, with a Ph.D. in linguistics, can decipher any hidden codes, messages, or foreign languages the Bureau sends her way, finding patterns where others cannot and making her indispensable in tracking down the most heinous of serial killers. In the Mojave Desert, a renowned archaeologist is found dead in a remote cave, surrounded by cryptic ancient symbols. Can Sofia unravel the complex web of secrets encoded within the glyphs before the killer claims his next victim?

"The plot has many twists and turns, but it is the ending, which I did not see coming at all, that totally defines this book as one of the most riveting that I have read in years."
—Reader review for Not Like Us

NO ONE LEFT is Book #2 in a long-anticipated new series by #1 bestseller Ava Strong, whose bestseller NOT LIKE US (a free download) has received over 1,000 five star ratings and reviews.

Born into a family of speech pathologists and raised with a unique heritage of German, Egyptian, and French roots, Sofia Blake has always appreciated diverse languages and cultures. With her exceptional language skills and natural talent for decoding cryptic messages, Sofia shot to the top ranks of the FBI. It seemed nothing could slow her down—until her travel-journalist sister mysteriously disappeared ten years ago.

Now, haunted by her past and desperate for answers, Sofia vows to use her extraordinary talents to stop more tragedies from occurring.

Is her linguistic genius enough to stop the vilest of killers?

Or will the killers reach her before she can crack their codes?

A page-turning crime thriller full of jaw-dropping twists and packed with heart-pounding suspense, the SOFIA BLAKE mystery series introduces a brilliant new female protagonist and will keep you on the edge of your seat. Fans of Rachel Caine, Teresa Driscoll, and Robert Dugoni are sure to fall in love.

More books in the series are also available!

"This is a chilling, suspenseful page turner that just might leave you scared at night!"
—Reader review for Not Like Us

"Very intriguing, kept me turning page after page… Lots of twists and turns and a very unexpected ending. Cannot wait for the next in this series!"
—Reader review for Not Like Us

"A roller coaster ride of events… Can't put down until you finish it!"
—Reader review for Not Like Us

"Excellent read with very realistic characters that you become emotionally invested in… Couldn't put it down!"
—Reader review for The Death Code

"An excellent read, lots of twists and turns, with a surprising ending, leaving you wanting to read the next book in the series! Well done!"
—Reader review for The Death Code

"Well worth the read. Cannot wait to see what happens in the next book!"
—Reader review for The Death Code

"Quickly became a story I couldn't put down! I highly recommend this book!"
—Reader review for His Other Wife

"I really enjoyed the fast-paced action, plot design and characterization... I didn't want to put the book down and the ending was a total surprise."
—Reader review for His Other Wife

"The characters are extremely well developed... There are twists and turns in the plot that kept me guessing. An extremely well written story."
—Reader review for His Other Wife

"One of the best books I have ever read... The ending was perfect and surprising. Ava Strong is an amazing writer."
—Reader review for His Other Wife

"Holy cow, what a rollercoaster... Many times I absolutely KNEW who the killer was—only to be proven wrong each time. I was completely surprised by the ending. I have to say, I am thrilled that this is the first in a series. My only complaint is that the next one isn't out yet. I need it!"
—Reader review for His Other Wife

"An incredible, intense, spellbinding, enjoyable story. It will keep you captivated until the end."
—Reader review for His Other Wife

Ava Strong

Ava Strong is author of the REMI LAURENT mystery series, comprising six books (and counting); of the ILSE BECK mystery series, comprising seven books (and counting); of the STELLA FALL psychological suspense thriller series, comprising six books (and counting); of the DAKOTA STEELE FBI suspense thriller series, comprising six books (and counting); of the LILY DAWN suspense thriller series, comprising five books (and counting); the MEGAN YORK FBI suspense thriller series, comprising five books (and counting); and the SOFIA BLAKE FBI suspense thriller series, comprising five books (and counting).

An avid reader and lifelong fan of the mystery and thriller genres, Ava loves to hear from you, so please feel free to visit www.avastrongauthor.com to learn more and stay in touch.

BOOKS BY AVA STRONG

MEGAN YORK FBI SUSPENSE THRILLER
YOU'LL BE SORRY (Book #1)
YOU'LL BE NEXT (Book #2)
YOU'LL BE MINE (Book #3)
YOU'LL BE FIRST (Book #4)
YOU'LL BE GONE (Book #5)

LILY DAWN FBI SUSPENSE THRILLER
STILL ALIVE (Book #1)
STILL HOPE (Book #2)
STILL AWAKE (Book #3)
STILL HERE (Book #4)
STILL MAD (Book #5)

REMI LAURENT FBI SUSPENSE THRILLER
THE DEATH CODE (Book #1)
THE MURDER CODE (Book #2)
THE MALICE CODE (Book #3)
THE VENGEANCE CODE (Book #4)
THE DECEPTION CODE (Book #5)
THE SEDUCTION CODE (Book #6)

ILSE BECK FBI SUSPENSE THRILLER
NOT LIKE US (Book #1)
NOT LIKE HE SEEMED (Book #2)
NOT LIKE YESTERDAY (Book #3)
NOT LIKE THIS (Book #4)
NOT LIKE SHE THOUGHT (Book #5)
NOT LIKE BEFORE (Book #6)
NOT LIKE NORMAL (Book #7)

STELLA FALL PSYCHOLOGICAL SUSPENSE THRILLER
HIS OTHER WIFE (Book #1)
HIS OTHER LIE (Book #2)
HIS OTHER SECRET (Book #3)
HIS OTHER MISTRESS (Book #4)
HIS OTHER LIFE (Book #5)

HIS OTHER TRUTH (Book #6)

DAKOTA STEELE FBI SUSPENSE THRILLER
WITHOUT MERCY (Book #1)
WITHOUT REMORSE (Book #2)
WITHOUT A PAST (Book #3)
WITHOUT PITY (Book #4)
WITHOUT HOPE (Book #5)

Made in United States
North Haven, CT
04 March 2024

49555139R00088